SERVICES RENDERED

The Cases of Dan Shamble, Zombie P.I.

Kevin J. Anderson

EBook ISBN: 978-1-61475-942-3
Trade Paperback ISBN: 978-1-61475-941-6
Dust Jacket Hardcover ISBN: 978-1-61475-943-0

Cover art/design by miblart
Art Director Kevin J. Anderson
Published by
WordFire Press, LLC
PO Box 1840
Monument CO 80132
Kevin J. Anderson & Rebecca Moesta, Publishers
WordFire Press eBook Edition 2022
WordFire Press Trade Paperback Edition 2022
WordFire Press Hardcover Edition 2022

Join our WordFire Press Readers Group for
sneak previews, updates, new projects, and giveaways.
Sign up at wordfirepress.com

CONTENTS

Paperwork

I t would have been a relatively quiet afternoon in the offices of Chambeaux & Deyer Investigations, if not for the pissed off poltergeist. The vengeful, rambunctious spirit released its malicious fury in the most heinous way possible—by attacking our filing cabinets.

As a zombie private detective, I do like a little action. I've been known to go running after mange-encrusted werewolves with my .38 drawn, holding my fedora to my head. Frankly, I just enjoy solving mysteries, whether they are actual crimes or just crossword puzzles.

We don't get a lot of business, even in the mayhem of the Unnatural Quarter, but whenever a case does come in, I really sink my teeth into it. (Not like *that*! I'm not one of those ill-mannered brain-eating zombies.) I follow the leads, interview the suspects, and use my imagination. I may have a hole in my head from the bullet that killed me, but I still have all of my P.I. smarts.

Some of the Chambeaux & Deyer clients don't involve mysteries to be solved. I'm the Dan Chambeaux half of the partnership (and don't call me "Shamble"; it sounds less professional). Robin Deyer, the passionate human lawyer who shares my offices, wants justice for all Unnaturals, and she gets cases just as bizarre as mine.

That's why the poltergeist was so pissed off. I didn't have anything to do with it. Honest.

Marisol Shanker was a human client, a quiet and modest woman who worked in the post office in the unclaimed relics section. The shipping of cursed items and unidentified body parts posed challenges to the normally sedate and inefficient postal service. Marisol had been contentedly, if not quite happily, married to her husband Randy for twelve years in a bland middle-class life, until Randy died of a heart attack while yelling at the TV, disputing an answer on his favorite game show.

Even more unfortunate than Randy's death was his return as a poltergeist who wouldn't leave his poor widow alone. His glowing spectral form still appeared every evening to lounge in his old recliner and watch his favorite TV shows. After their twelve years of marriage, however, Marisol realized that Randy's favorite TV shows weren't necessarily *her* favorite TV shows. Since it was now her own home, she kept changing the channel to the programs she preferred to watch. As a poltergeist, Randy kept changing the channel back.

The breaking point came after two years when Marisol decided she wanted to move on with her life and start dating again. Randy's poltergeist didn't appreciate that, and manifested himself to wreak havoc, overturning restaurant tables, spilling wine bottles, emitting sounds like loud cell phone ringtones in quiet movie theaters. He ruined every single first date she had, and Marisol never received any offers for second dates.

Distraught, she had come to Chambeaux & Deyer, begging Robin for help. "I need a restraining order," Marisol said, wringing her hands.

Robin has soulful dark brown eyes and a very understanding expression, which can turn into legal steel once she becomes a client's advocate. "Tell me about it, Ms. Shanker."

"I didn't ask to become a widow, but it is what it is. I want to find a nice man to keep me company for the rest of my life," she said. "And Randy has to move on, too. I don't mind if he finds another nice ghost of his own." Marisol glanced over at Sheyenne's beautiful spectral form at the reception desk.

Sheyenne, my ghost girlfriend and office manager, is all business and offers invaluable advice, but she never misses a chance to flirt with me. That's how you keep a relationship strong, even after death did us part.

"I'm taken," she said, beaming at me. "And so is Dan."

Disconcerted, Marisol said, "I'm sure there must be some kind of spiritual singles service in the Quarter?"

"In fact there is. We worked a case with them once, the Monster Match dating service." I smiled as I recalled that case, which had involved a beauty pageant, a Medusa, and—

Robin interrupted. "First, we have to keep you safe, Ms. Shanker. I'll file a restraining order right away, and your husband will have to leave you alone. He might not like it, but the court system is more powerful than poltergeist powers."

Relieved, Marisol dabbed at her eyes with a wadded tissue. "As soon as you possibly can. I have another date next Tuesday with a really nice man."

"Once the paperwork is filed, Randy can't come anywhere near you. You'll be safe and protected." Robin patted her wrist reassuringly. Sheyenne gave the client a soulful smile that made my undead heart want to beat again.

"You can trust Chambeaux and Deyer, ma'am," I told her.

The case was simple and straightforward, barely worth writing down. Within a day, Robin had served the restraining order, which prevented the disturbingly tangible spirit of Randy Shanker from bothering his widow, and she was free to go on her blind date. Happily ever after.

Alas, Robin had forgotten to include *our offices* in the restraining order, and so the vengeful spirit came after us instead, as if hell had frozen over and he had forgotten his ice skates.

Our office door was closed for the lunch hour, but ghosts don't have to knock. Randy the poltergeist made a point of solidifying himself enough to shatter the marbled glass window as he flung himself into the offices, spitting curses that made my ears burn, swear words that he must have heard in the fifth pit of hell. Randy rampaged through the office, spinning the chairs around, making the fluorescent lights flicker more than usual, overturning the plastic potted plant.

Robin and I both ran out of our offices, wondering what the tumult was all about. Sheyenne shouted at the poltergeist, "You can't be in here! We're closed for lunch." He responded by calling her names that even demons wouldn't use in polite company.

Out of spite, he flung himself upon our file cabinets. Metal drawers flew open with a loud clang. Manila folders sprayed in the air like playing cards from a shuffling machine. All our carefully organized cases, the detailed notes, the depositions, the coffee receipts, became a blizzard of documents.

Sheyenne was a big girl and she had a thick skin, metaphorically speaking, and she could put aside the insults that made me so furious. What she couldn't abide, however, was someone messing with her filing system. "You stop that this instant!"

The poltergeist swelled up and I could imagine his last moments when he had burst out of his recliner to yell at the TV strenuously enough to initiate a heart attack. He inflated himself in an attempt to look fearsome.

Sheyenne was not impressed—and her well-practiced poltergeist powers were far superior to his.

As Robin and I watched helplessly, the two ghosts reeled in the air in a knock-down, drag-out fight for the soul of the office. Their glowing forms ricocheted against the walls, banged into the file cabinets, and rattled more paperwork loose. Sheyenne's perfect blond hair didn't even get messed up as she clawed and kicked. She manifested herself solidly enough to rip into Randy and frighten the intangible crap out of him.

"You want something worse than a restraining order?" Sheyenne said. "Come back and face me!" She shoved him hard with the hands that had so delicately caressed my chest back in the good old days, when we were both alive.

Randy tumbled in the air, hurtled straight for our second-story window. I cringed, expecting to hear glass break, but instead the poltergeist passed right though the wall to the left of the window and spilled out into the air, dropping slowly to the streets like a puff of vengeful dandelion fluff.

Sheyenne flitted to the window and shouted, "Don't you ever come back! Leave your wife alone and stay out of trouble." She wrenched down the window with her insubstantial hands, slamming it shut. "Case closed."

Sheyenne drifted over to me, and her glowing presence softened. "Oh, Beaux. That was scary."

I pretended to wrap my arms around her, even though she remained intangible to me. "Yes, you were."

"Excellent work, Sheyenne," Robin said. "I'll amend the restraining order to include our offices as well."

"Probably not necessary," I replied. "That poltergeist will never show his ectoplasm around here again."

With a quiet groan, Sheyenne looked around the disheveled mess of the office, the file folders strewn about as if a hyperactive blind man had been in a race to alphabetize them.

With perfect bad timing, Officer Toby McGoohan appeared at the door and looked through the shattered pane. He reached through the jagged opening and turned the inner door handle to let himself in. "Hey, Shamble. Did you know your glass is broken?"

"Thanks, McGoo," I said. "We hadn't noticed."

McGoo, my Best Human Friend, will likely never be promoted above beat cop because he doesn't know how to keep his foot out of his mouth. He crossed his arms over his blue policeman's uniform and looked at the explosion of files. "Whoa, I thought I hated paperwork."

"We're glad you came to help, Officer McGoohan," Robin said. "You were involved in almost all of these cases. You can help us sort through them."

He scratched his freckled cheek. "I could ..." He let his voice trail off as he looked at me. "Do I at least get a beer out of it, Shamble?"

"A beer? Lunch hour isn't even over," I said. "We'll get you one of those sissy cinnamon lattes you like so much."

McGoo blushed. "Don't tell people that's what I drink! It's not manly."

"Damn right it's not," I said. Sheyenne snickered.

He huffed, "It better be a venti, then." He bent down to pick up a manila folder at his feet. "Hey, I remember this one, the case with the book collector and the cursed paperbacks."

I scooped an armful of manila folders and dropped them on Sheyenne's desk. I sorted through them, skimming the cases. "And here's the one-eyed newt and the cooking competition."

Robin chuckled, "That was a good one. I've got the Mayan sacrificial Christmas turkey right here."

Sheyenne used her poltergeist powers to rearrange the papers, straightening an entire stack and pulling out a sheet that didn't belong with the others. "This one's about Headless Guy. I hope he's still all right."

Robin neatly put together another folder and handed it to Sheyenne for proper filing. "This is the case of the genies and the missing werewolf boy."

"Don't forget the toolbox and the dimensional door-way," I said.

Robin sniffed. "Of course not. That goes without saying."

With her blue eyes sparkling, Sheyenne said, "This is a thick file, the wild west outlaw ghosts and your duel at high midnight."

McGoo patted his chest as if looking for bullet holes there. "I'll never forget that one."

Although we started out with determination and a great deal of energy, as we sorted through the cases, we found ourselves spending more and more time reading and reminiscing. It was as much fun reliving those old adventures as it was to have new ones. As I said, it was a slow afternoon.

These records were a testament to our hard work, imagination, and, more often than not, blind luck. As I always say, the cases don't solve themselves. Sometimes you need a zombie private investigator.

And all of his sidekicks.

Eye of Newt

I

The afternoon got a lot more interesting when the one-eyed lizard guy stumbled into our offices, begging for protection.

At Chambeaux & Deyer Investigations, even on quiet days, there's always paperwork to do, files to close out, dead cases to resurrect or just bury for good. I'm a detective—a zombie detective. I can throw a mean punch and stand up to the ugliest, foulest-smelling demon ... but paperwork was never my forte. That's why I have an office assistant, Sheyenne. She's a ghost, and she's also my girlfriend. It doesn't matter that we intermingle our work lives and our personal lives, since neither of us is alive anyway.

Sheyenne had been re-alphabetizing files while I looked over cases I had recently wrapped up, some in more dramatic fashion than others, a few even verging on "end of the world" dramatic, so it's a good thing I'm skilled at my job. In studying the files, I wasn't looking for mistakes, just reviewing my greatest hits and wishing we had another case to work on at the moment.

My lawyer partner, Robin Deyer, was in court prosecuting a case of cemeterial fraud and incompetence—an underclass action suit against a tombstone engraver who had committed far too many misspellings. Now that zombies were rising frequently from the grave, the formerly silent customers noticed the typos in their headstones, and a group had hired Robin to sue for damages on their behalf.

That left just Sheyenne and me in the offices. We had a dinner date planned for that evening, but we hadn't settled on a restaurant yet. It was mainly an excuse for us to be together, all form and no sustenance, since I rarely ate anyway and a ghost didn't eat at all.

In the meantime, as she flitted from one file cabinet to another, Sheyenne watched a small TV tuned to a local cable channel that covered the Stone Cold Monster Cookoff, which was taking place downtown in the Unnatural Quarter. A variety of skilled chefs competed in a days' long event; the crowds were getting larger now that the cookoff was down to three finalists. Sheyenne watched the unnatural chefs go about their extravagant preparations with enough pots, pans, and utensils to equip an inhuman army. She jotted down a recipe suggested by the loud, green-skinned Ragin' Cajun Mage, just in case she ever got around to cooking.

Then the office door crashed open, which was all the more remarkable because the creature that barged in was barely three feet tall. A scrawny lizard man with speckled brown skin, one yellow eye, and gauze and surgical tape covering where the other eye should have been.

"I need your help!" he said, in a phlegmy, hissy voice. "Are you, Dan Shamble? You've got to help me!"

"It's *Chambeaux*," I corrected him as I came out of my office to greet him. I moved stiffly on joints that were still recovering from rigor mortis.

Sheyenne is usually very professional, but she cried out in delight when she saw him. "Oh, aren't you cute! Look, Beaux—he's from the car insurance commercials."

After stumbling inside, the lizard man slammed the door behind him with surprising strength. "That's a gecko," he snapped. His long tongue flicked in and out. "I'm a *newt*. There's a difference."

"Sorry if I offended you." She drifted forward to meet him. "Come in, sir. You're safe here."

I made sure my .38 was in its hip holster just in case the lizard man was being imminently pursued, but when no slavering eye-stealing monsters charged after him, I figured we had enough time for a normal client intake meeting. "Tell me what's going on, Mr., uh, Newt."

"My name is Geck." That must have been embarrassing for a guy who was too often confused for a humorous gecko insurance spokesman. "There's a hit out on me, and I was attacked last night."

"Who, exactly, is out to get you?"

He shook his head. "I don't know! I didn't think I had any enemies. I mean, I'm a warm and fuzzy guy … as far as an amphibian can be."

In the conference room I had to bring him a booster

chair so he could see over the edge of the table. If Robin were here, she would have been taking copious notes on a yellow legal pad, but I just sat and listened. The one-eyed newt didn't seem at all bothered by the bullet hole in the center of my forehead, or my gray pallor. "Tell us your story, Geck."

He licked his lips. "I'm walking home, minding my own business, whistling to myself, and then ..." He shuddered. "Suddenly, I get accosted by two big thugs—a rock monster and a clay golem. 'Get him! He's the one we've got a contract out on,' says the rock monster, and the golem says, 'Don't end a sentence with a preposition.'

"And they grab me. Because it's a cool night, I'm a little lethargic. If I'd been sunning myself on a hot rock, I could've scurried out of their grasp, but I was too slow. They grab me, slam me up against the brick wall of an alley, then ... they take out a long spoon." He shuddered again, sobbed. "They scoop out my eye, quick as you please, and pop it in a glass bottle. The golem holds me while the rock monster just laughs! 'We'd get twice as much if we took your other eye, too,' he says. 'You better watch yourself.' Then the golem says, 'He won't be watching much of anything now. Come on, we got what we need.'"

The newt self-consciously touched the wadded bandages on his face. "Then they went away and left me there. The golem seemed guilty, even sorry, but the rock monster was just mean."

"I'm not surprised," I said. "Rock monsters tend to be

hard and grumbly, while golems are made of clay, so they are softer in general."

"What am I going to do?" Geck wailed. "If there's still a hit out on me, someone might try to take my other eye. I'm not safe."

I knew I could take him down to the precinct and ask for protective custody from my BHF, my Best Human Friend, Officer Toby McGoohan, but that would be only a temporary solution, and this needed more direct intervention.

"We have to find out who took out a contract on you," I said. "Learn what you did, and try to make amends. Do you have *any idea* who it was? Who's got a grudge against you? Do you owe money?"

"Any idea at all?" Sheyenne pressed, hovering close to him.

Geck hung his head. He looked ill, although I knew the greenish-brown tinge to his hide was probably natural. "Only the library comes to mind. I think I've seen the rock monster and the golem there—they sometimes work as security guards. And I do have an overdue book and a fine." He blinked his remaining eye. "You don't think … ?"

Even Sheyenne paled, and I steeled myself. "You don't mess with the Spider Lady of the Unnatural Quarter Public Library. Everyone knows that." This was going to be a more dangerous case than I had expected. "We'd better go face her—in person, you and me, and see if we can resolve this. You won't be safe until you're off her hit list."

II

Geck and I headed through town toward the Unnatural Quarter Public Library main branch and Vault of Secrets. We made a side trip to his dank lair, a communal sub-basement where other newts shared the rent, with mud and moss for carpeting and a steady drip through the ceiling for running water. Not a good place to keep an overdue library book, I thought. At least he had it on a high shelf, away from the drip. Geck hauled over a stepstool so he could retrieve it.

"So, tell me about this book you checked out," I said. "How long is it overdue, and why is it so important?"

"A month overdue … I kept putting it off, Mr. Shamble. And then it got worse, and the fines built up." He held the thick volume close.

"How much?"

"Ten bucks."

"Better take twenty. We may need to pay off the Spider Lady, but we'll get you back on the straight and narrow."

He looked down at the heavy volume that seemed too big for him to carry. For the sake of efficiency, I took it from him, and we set off, while two other newts were waiting to stand under the ceiling drip for a shower.

"Never even finished it." Geck sounded guilty. "I went to the library for something to read in a puddle on a sunny day. I really enjoyed all the Harry Potter books, and I heard that the Harry Dresden novels by Jim Butcher were excellent, but they were all checked out.

"Then somebody said Shakespeare in the same sentence with Butcher, so I decided to look into that Shakespeare guy as my second choice. The only copy available was a rare special edition, *The Complete Pre-Humous Writings of William Shakespeare*. It was even autographed."

I frowned, knowing that someone who purported to be Shakespeare's ghost had been publishing new posthumously written plays and sonnets, but his claim had been debunked. He was, in fact, just another aspiring ghost writer with a good costume and literary airs, but apparently the library hadn't caught up yet.

"I tried to read the Shakespeare stuff, but I couldn't get into it," the newt said. "It wasn't like Harry Potter at all. It was boring. But I kept trying ... and then the book was late, and I felt guilty, so I kept trying to read it. The fines piled up, and then I started getting threatening letters, so I was afraid to come to the library. And then ..." He self-consciously touched the bandages covering his right eye.

"You need to bring the book back, and you'll have to make amends to the librarian," I said. "That may be the only way we can keep you intact, more or less. When we get to the library, let me do the talking. And bring your twenty bucks."

On our way across the Quarter, we passed vampires sitting outside under sun umbrellas at a blood bar. Two werewolf women offered discounts on "full claw treatment" pedicures. A mummy rode by on a bicycle, wobbling and unbalanced; he was taken completely off guard when one of his unraveled bandages caught in the chain, and he and the bicycle tumbled into the gutter.

We passed the Ghoul's Diner, where I often liked to sit at the counter with an abysmally bad cup of coffee and a disgusting miasma of a daily special. The diner and its unfortunate food were upstaged now, however, as the entire block had been barricaded off for the final rounds of the Stone Cold Monster Cookoff. A grandstand had been set up for the culinary acrobatics, and spectators gathered around, hoping for—or dreading—free samples.

I assumed the diner's business had suffered due to the event, but the ghoul proprietor never seemed to pay much attention to the outside world or his customers. It was business as usual.

In fact, everyone in the Unnatural Quarter—monsters and humans—got along about as well as anybody got along in the rest of the world. Ever since the Big Uneasy more than a decade ago, the world had been settling down from the change. The event had been caused by a strange alignment of planets and a completely coincidental spilling of virgin's blood on an original copy of the *Necronomicon*, which resulted in cosmic upheavals, rifts in the universal continuum, a shift in reality.

But after all that was over, naturals and unnaturals had to learn how to coexist, and everyday life returned with surprising stability. It could have been a real zombie apocalypse, but it wasn't so much an apocalypse as an awkward reunion.

Back then, I was a private investigator who hadn't seen much success in the real world, but I found a whole new clientele among the unnaturals. My business partner Robin joined me because she insisted that downtrodden unnaturals needed legal representation, too. Everything had been going fine—until one of my cases went south, and I ended up being shot in the back of the head.

These days, that isn't quite as final as it might sound. I rose from the grave and got right back on the case, eventually solving my own murder, then moving on.

It goes to show how much the world has settled into a new normal if a crowd of naturals and unnaturals can get excited about a cookoff championship.

Up on stage, after a round of digestive elimination, the Stone Cold culinary marathon had settled on its three finalists. On the left side of the grandstand was Leatherneck, a burly man in a leather apron, leather mask, and upright shocks of greasy hair. He used a rusty shovel to scoop mangled animal remains into the hopper of a meat grinder that was about the size of a wood chipper.

"To make Texas chainsaw chili," he said, "any sort of road kill will do—as long as it's been seasoned with hot sun and asphalt for at least four days."

The meat grinder whirred and spat out a brownish-red paste flecked with hair and fur that glopped into an already bubbling cauldron. The big chef added a pinch of salt, bent over to sniff the pot, then held up a gigantic razor-edged butcher knife. He raised his left forearm, which was a network of white scars. Without flinching, Leatherneck drew the blade down his forearm, opening up a wide gash that bled profusely into the pot. He held his arm over the chili as red dripped into the sauce, then with bright eyes behind his leather mask, he said, "And now for the special ingredient." The crowd fell into a hush, and the big man lifted up a jar of green spices with his non-bleeding arm. *"Oregano!"* He sprinkled a third of the jar into his pot.

The vampires in the audience had become extremely attentive when they watched him shed blood for his chili, but the oregano left them with sour frowns.

Next up was a heavyset, matronly woman whose beehive hair had a white lightning stripe, like the bride of Frankenstein. Her skin was chalky and pale, but her eyes were fiery red. Sheyenne sometimes watched her TV show, "Kitchen Litch," and she complained that the Kitchen Litch considered herself superior to her viewers. "The sort of person who would say 'tomaaahto coulis' instead of ketchup," Sheyenne had described her.

The Kitchen Litch held a large sauté pan over a gas burner. "Every ingredient must be frrrresh," she said with an exaggerated roll of her r's. "First, we start with clarified butter." She ladled a greasy yellow pool into the pan, then reached inside a wicker basket, rummaging around. "And the frrreshest of frrresh is an ingredient that is … *alive!*"

She pulled out a black beetle as large as her hand. It squirmed and thrashed, but she threw it onto the sizzling pan. "And I always keep a special container of fresh blood-sucking gnats for garnish, but that will be for the finish." She reached into the basket to grab another beetle, while the first beetle flopped and hopped, dancing on the hot pan surface. Its black carapace cracked open, and it buzzed its wings to fly away.

"No, no!" The Kitchen Litch swatted with a spatula as the second skittering beetle also tried to take flight. She smashed that one into a pulp, and it sizzled in a little beetle patty in the frying pan. The first beetle, though, got away, winging up from the stage. Three more beetles escaped from the still-open wicker basket, and the flustered Kitchen Litch slammed the lid back down. Trying to recover her composure, she said to the audience, "Of course, frrresh ingredients also pose certain challenges." She busied herself nursing the beetle patty with her spatula.

The third chef, a loud green-skinned man, the Ragin' Cajun Mage, cooked flamboyantly beside two large glass aquariums filled with thrashing ingredients. He looked at the Kitchen Litch with scorn. "I agree with my incompetent rival—fresh ingredients are key, but so are *secret* ingredients, and I have about a dozen secret ingredients."

The Cajun Mage rapped his knuckles against the aquariums filled with silty gray-brown water. Swarms of thrashing tentacles writhed at him like a wrestling match between a squid and an octopus. Armored claws clacked in another aquarium. "We have a live mutant crawdad tank and a live assorted-tentacles tank. They'll wait, though, until my nightmare étouffée is ready. It takes half a day to simmer properly. First, we make a nice roux, starting with some perfect sassafras filé." He dumped a gray-green powder into the bottom of his stockpot. "Then some toadstool filé."

His eyes twinkled as he lifted up a crystalline vial. "And for the perfect seasoning, the tears of heartbroken girls. Two tablespoons will do." He poured the vial into the pot, then whisked it around as he increased the heat.

Geck and I had paused to watch the show. The smells wafting around the grandstand were an odd mix of appetizing and disgusting. My client glanced around the crowd, fidgeting and nervous, as if afraid someone might attack him right there out in the open, but I was sure he would be safe here. The Spider Lady from the library would not make a move on him at the Monster Cookoff. She had already delivered her ominous message.

One of the escaped black beetles buzzed through the air toward us, wobbling like a drunken bumblebee. Geck's yellow eye brightened, and he swiveled his salamander-like head, poised, tense ... then he lashed out with his tongue. But he missed the beetle entirely, which buzzed away unaffected.

Geck groaned. "Bloody depth perception! I'm going to starve!"

As the green-skinned Cajun Mage moved to the next stage of his highly complex recipe, I nudged the newt along. "Come on, then. It's off to the library. This is a matter of life or death."

III

The Unnatural Quarter Public Library and Vault of Secrets was not meant to be a terrifying place, but Geck looked as if he would rather have been going to the dentist —and I didn't even know if newts had teeth.

The large stone building was impressive in one sense, looming in another sense. A poster in one of the dust-specked windows said, "Come for fun in the library!" in blood-dripping letters. Because the stone steps were so widely spaced, I had to help Geck up each one.

As we climbed to the pillared entrance, he seemed

more and more nervous. "You have to face this," I said. "If we can resolve your overdue library book, the Spider Lady will take you off her hit list, then you won't have to worry anymore." The newt swallowed and moved on.

At the top of the broad steps, two fierce-looking stone lions crouched on pedestals. Just as we reached the top of the platform, a nervous-looking vampire scuttled out of the library entrance with a book hidden under his arm— and the two stone lions woke up. The ferocious living statues snorted, snarled, and rose on their heavy paws.

The nervous vampire clutched his book and scuttled backward, looking from side to side, trapped. One lion bounded off its pedestal and pinned him to the ground. He flailed and screamed. "I'll check out the book, I promise. I'll check it out!"

The vampire had been trying to smuggle out a hard-cover copy of *Twilight*.

With a snort, the stone lion smacked the vampire and sent him careening back into the library. Though uninjured, he was extremely embarrassed to have his reading material revealed.

The incident did little to calm Geck's nerves. I tried to reassure him. "I'm here to protect you and negotiate on your behalf." I did not point out that even the most highly skilled zombie P.I. could do little to protect against giant stone lions or demonic head librarians.

The main library smelled of books, that weighty, dusty aroma that always brings back nostalgic memories. The patrons included humans, particularly college students doing reports on the social changes brought on by the Big

Uneasy. Mummy scholars worked with large stacks of papyrus, jotting down notes in hieroglyphics. Vampires developed family trees, while full-furred werewolves stood muttering together in the Pets section.

On the high shelves, accessible only by rickety ladders that looked more dangerous than the evil spell books themselves, a cleaning crew of goblins skittered about stringing cobwebs. In the middle of the floor, two large spinner racks held paperback bestsellers.

Geck looked around nervously, scanning the library. He whispered, "I don't see the rock monster or the golem. They're usually guarding the doors. Maybe they're off stealing someone else's eye."

"Or maybe it's their day off," I said.

"Or, maybe they're waiting to pounce on me again! Keep your eyes open, Mr. Shamble. You have more of them than I do."

At the main reference desk sat a withered, prim old woman who looked as if she suffered from chronic hemorrhoids. Her hair was pulled back into a bun so tight she didn't need a facelift, and she wore cat's-eye glasses that were large enough to be used as a weapon. She scanned the library like a high-tech targeting system, and when a young college couple began talking too loud, she suddenly reached out with a freakishly long, multi-jointed arm that held a ruler. Even though they were twenty feet away, she rapped on the table in front of them. "Quiet please in the library!" The old woman folded her extra arm back down under the desk.

Her nameplate said, "Hi, I'm Frieda. I'm here to help."

I nudged Geck, and we walked up to the desk. The newt was far too short, and I had to lift him up so he could meet the cat's-eye glasses with his remaining eye.

I looked behind the counter and saw that Frieda the Spider Lady had a nest of additional multi-jointed limbs all curled up beneath her flower-print dress. One set of hands was typing, while another paged through a printed book; behind her, two more limbs reached out to pluck volumes off a shelving cart. She gave us part of her attention. "How may I help you?"

"I'm Dan Chambeaux, Private Investigator, ma'am, and this newt is my client, Geck. I'm afraid there's been some misunderstanding, and I'm here to help resolve it."

The librarian frowned. "Misunderstanding? If words and sentences were stated clearly, there would be no misunderstandings."

"My library book is late," Geck blurted out, sounding ashamed.

The Spider Lady practically recoiled, as if he had hurled a terrible insult at her. "That changes things. Substantially."

I interjected, holding up the Shakespeare Pre-Humous Writings volume I had carried from his dank quarters. "My client has incurred library fines, which he is willing to pay, so long as he stops receiving threatening letters from the library. As you can see, he has already suffered a great deal of physical harm." I used my "be reasonable" voice, which rarely worked against villains; even so, the detective training handbook suggested being reasonable as a first step.

Frieda's voice was filled with venom. "And what is this book? How valuable is it?" Beneath the counter, her hidden limbs twitched. Many of them ended in claws. "And how despicable are you?"

Geck stammered and held out a rumpled receipt, while I slid over the book. The Spider Lady nudged her cat's-eye glasses, and her face seemed to wither even more. "This was part of our special Shakespeare collection—do you have any idea what sort of damage you've done? How many college treatises have been delayed because the authors had no access to this wonderful tome?"

"I ... I'm sorry."

"And it's autographed too!" said Freda, as if that were the last nail in the coffin.

"You do realize that the autograph is fake, ma'am?" I pointed out, hoping that might mitigate her ire. "The author of the posthumous works is not the real Shakespeare's ghost."

The librarian sniffed. "It's still of historical and popular interest." She shuffled papers and withdrew a formal parchment document that looked like a death sentence decree. A dozen names were written on it, seven of which had been crossed off, as if terminated.

Geck the Newt was on the list, third from the bottom. "I'm sorry, I'm sorry!" he blubbered, then quickly slapped a moist and rumpled twenty on the counter next to her nameplate. "I'll pay the fine—I'll pay double!—just please don't send your goons after me. Don't take my other eye!"

Now it was the Spider Lady's turn to look off balance. "Take your other eye? Why on earth would I wish to do that? My sole reason for existence is to *encourage reading*. If I took your other eye, that would be against my principles, although the library does have a large selection of unabridged audiobooks."

I stood up for Geck. "My client was recently accosted in an alley by a rock monster and a golem, both of whom are known to work here in the library. If you didn't send them to steal his eye, then who did?"

The Spider Lady seemed flustered. "You must mean Rocky and Ned. They're just part-time contract security guards. It's so hard to find good security guards in the Unnatural Quarter—they tend to suffer unfortunate ends. But I had to let Rocky and Ned go. I caught them eating in the library, which is inexcusable."

She snatched the bill and used one folded arm to squirrel it away in a small cashbox, while another arm took the book and stacked it on the shelving cart behind her. With a third hand, she stamped PAID on her hit list next to Geck's name.

She reached out with another one of her long arms and slapped a zombie reader who had unconsciously folded down the corner of a page in order to mark his place. "Damage to library property! I *will* write you up."

I got her attention again. "If you didn't put out a contract to take my client's eye, then who did?"

"How should I know that?"

I indicated the sign on the desk. "It says you're a reference librarian."

"I'm afraid you'll have to do your own research, Mr. Shamble. You might begin by asking whether this action was a punitive measure against Geck specifically, or if someone actually needed the eye for some other purpose."

IV

I knew we could get worthwhile advice from the Unorthodox Lab Equipment and Organ Boutique, a small specialty business that catered to a broad clientele ranging from hobbyist mad scientists to evil corporate research centers with underground monster-development programs.

An imp named Gunther managed the place and kept all his wares in total disorganization on the shelves, like a secret code that only he knew how to interpret. His business had picked up dramatically after the demise of Tony Cralo's Body Parts Emporium, a giant organ superstore run by an obese zombie mobster. After I had exposed Cralo to justice, his business completely collapsed. Score one for the good guys. That annoyed many of the Quarter's mad scientists, however, because they could no longer do one-stop shopping.

The little imp was climbing a set of shelves and stacking glass jars filled with specimens preserved in formaldehyde. The jars themselves were as big as the diminutive imp, but he was strong. Gunther nearly lost his grip on a jar filled with intestines labeled with a sticker that said *Great for decorating!*

Seeing us, he swung down with simian agility and dropped with flat feet on the countertop. His gaze turned immediately toward the newt, focusing on the bandages.

"Looks like somebody's in the market for a new eye! I have a wide selection." He clucked his pointed tongue. "I'll have to take socket measurements, though. Would you like to match the original color, or should we try something more fashionable?"

Geck said, "I'd rather have my own eye back—and I want to keep the one I still have."

When I explained how my client had been attacked, the imp proprietor seemed very disturbed. "The Unnatural Quarter is going down the tubes. Sure, people used to get roofied and wake up in hotel bathtubs missing a kidney or two, but that was just an expected part of the business. Taking an eye right out on the streets?" The imp shook his head in disgust.

"Have you had any customers asking for an eye of newt?" I asked.

"Not in particular. Sure, newt eyes are rare, but I have a selection of perfectly adequate toad eyes and salamander eyes. They'll do in a pinch." He clucked his pointed tongue again, touching Geck's bandages. "I could make do, find something that'll fit you, though it might look a little odd. Any decent scientist could install one, so long as it's in good condition."

"But is there a reason why someone would particularly want Geck's eye?" I asked. "What are newt eyes used for?"

"I used mine for seeing," Geck snapped.

"I meant what would someone else use it for."

The imp pondered. "Various organs have potent sorcerous aspects, particularly the organs of magical creatures. Livers, spleens, pituitary glands, testicles, and the like. Rare, ancient magic books listed eye of newt as a vital ingredient for every sorcerer to have in the pantry, but it was never used to work magic. Those tomes weren't spell books." Gunther gave an impish grin. "They were recipes, you see."

"Recipes?" Wheels began to turn in my mind.

"Yes," said the imp. "Eye of newt is primarily used in cooking."

With a sinking feeling in the pit of my stomach, like the aftereffects of a bad pepperoni pizza, I hurried with the newt back to the Unnatural Quarter's Stone Cold Monster Cookoff.

We bumped into Officer Toby McGoohan, who was walking the beat and presumably maintaining order. The only orders, though, were being taken by shuffling zombie waitresses at the outside tables of the Ghoul's Diner.

"Hey, Shamble!" McGoo tipped his blue patrolman's cap. "Just another day on the job. There've been reports of culinary unrest." He nodded toward the grandstand where the three finalist chefs were finishing their hours-long preparations for their masterpiece dishes. Runners dispersed small samples among the spectators, who would then vote on the winner. No doubt there was illicit gambling, bookies taking bets as well as exchanging family recipes.

"If the wrong person wins, McGoo, there'll be some digestive upset among the crowd."

I noticed he was eating something wrapped in dripping paper, a meal from one of the food carts that catered to the human audience members: a hot dog that was wrapped in bacon and stuffed inside a glazed jelly donut. McGoo took a bite, then frowned at the show on stage. "I don't know how anybody can eat that stuff." He wiped the congealing mess from his lips.

"We already have enough to make our stomachs queasy, McGoo. A couple of thugs roughed up my client, Mr. Geck. They took his eye last night. At first we thought it was payback for an overdue library book, a contract taken out on him by the Spider Lady herself."

McGoo paled, which made the freckles on his cheeks seem more prominent. "The Spider Lady?"

I held up a hand. "But it wasn't that. We think these thugs *stole* Geck's eye ... for some nefarious purpose."

"There's always some nefarious purpose. Did you get a description of the perps?"

"Just general details. One's a rock monster, the other's a golem. Names are Ned and Rocky."

"That's enough to go on." McGoo pursed his lips. "I've been patrolling the crowd here. Lots of spectators, but I think I noticed that rock monster ... now that you mention it, he was with a golem. They were sitting at one of the outdoor tables at the Ghoul's Diner. I only noticed them because the rock monster was eating a bagel—a *toasted onion* bagel, but with *strawberry* cream cheese on it." He frowned. "That's the sort of thing an attentive cop will notice."

To the roar of the crowd, Leatherneck ladled out

samples of his Texas chainsaw chili, passing small cups around the crowd. He had reopened the big gash on his forearm so he could spruce up each bowl with a splash of blood. The vampire spectators crowded forward, eager to get their sample even with the addition of oregano to the pot. The persistent Kitchen Litch had managed to fricassee enough of the large beetles that she was prepared to serve, though she had not yet garnished the meal with her blood-sucking gnats.

The three of us hurried off to the diner at the edge of the cookoff crowd. Albert Gould had set up rickety card tables and temporary benches to take advantage of the additional customers, even though they were all watching the cookoff. McGoo pointed, "There's the bagel!"

I did see the onion bagel covered with strawberry cream cheese—which was certainly out of the ordinary—being held by a lumpy rock monster, a creature composed of assembled stones and a large yawning mouth just made to pulverize bagels. Next to him sat a gray clay golem sipping a tiny cup of espresso. I was shocked because I hadn't known the Ghoul's Diner served espresso.

Geck hopped up and down, trying to see. "That's them!"

On the stage with his big booming laugh, the green-skinned Ragin' Cajun Mage stirred his cauldron of night-mare étouffée. "Almost finished! Enjoy those other morsels while you can—and be prepared to surrender your taste buds to the Mage."

McGoo and I stepped up to the table, interrupting the rock monster and the golem. I tried to be as tough and determined as a zombie detective can be. "Are you Rocky? We'd like to have a word with you."

The rock monster turned its blocky head so I could see blazing red eyes deep within cave-like sockets. "I'm *Ned*. He's Rocky." He gestured to the golem, then took another big grinding bite of his bagel.

"We need to talk with both of you," I said.

McGoo puffed up his chest. "We've heard reports that you assaulted a citizen of the Quarter."

"Me, me!" said Geck, bouncing up and down. The newt was so short he didn't come up to the edge of the table, and the two thugs hadn't noticed him. I gave him a hand, lifting him up so the two could see him. "You stole my eye!"

"You got proof of that?" grumbled the rock monster. "It was dark in that alley. How can you be sure it was us?"

"So, you admit you were there," McGoo said.

Rocky the golem said, "Considering this person's condition, he's unreliable as an *eye*-witness."

Ned the rock monster snickered.

"It was them!" Geck said. "I'd point them out in a lineup any day of the week."

The rock monster rose to his feet, towering over us. "We took a job, we got paid. We're just blue-collar workers."

Rocky stood up to join him. "A golem is required to follow whatever commands a master issues, even a temporary master. There's been a legal precedent. We're not responsible for whatever we allegedly did or didn't do."

Ned added, "Besides, five bucks is five bucks."

"And assault on a newt is still considered assault," said McGoo. "I'm going to have to—"

Geck suddenly cried out as he jumped onto the table, disturbing the tiny cup of espresso and knocking the half-eaten bagel to the ground. "Look, look! That's my eye!"

On stage, the Ragin' Cajun Mage stood over his noisome vat of nightmare étouffée. He tried to impart a sense of awe on the spectators. "And the last, the rarest, the most special secret ingredient—not available at stores! —we add for the finish, *eye of newt!*"

The crowd gasped.

Geck shrieked.

The green-skinned Cajun chef dangled the vial containing the stolen amphibian eye and let the silence hang for a long and dangerous moment. Even the large aquariums of live mutated crawdads and live assorted tentacles thrashed and churned, either applauding or dreading the imminent moment when they would become part of the cooking performance.

"That's my eye!" Geck yelled again and bounded toward the stage.

The crowd stopped munching on their fricasseed beetle samples or Texas chainsaw chili. Many dropped their cups on the ground.

McGoo withdrew his service revolver and pointed it at the Ragin' Cajun Mage. "Stop right there! That eyeball is private property. Everyone else, stay calm."

Of course the spectators panicked.

Knowing the crowd could turn ugly—well, the crowd was already ugly, but it could get worse—I pointed at the golem and the rock monster. They were both mercenaries to the core. "Five bucks if you help us resolve this," I offered.

"Each?" asked Ned.

I hesitated only a second and considered it a worthwhile investment. "Each."

The two large, gray forms lumbered into the crowd.

The newt dashed up onto the stage with the speed of a sun-warmed lizard. Geck threw himself with a full fury at the Cajun Mage, attempting to tackle him and seize his eye before it fell into the cauldron of étouffée. Alas, unaccustomed to his lack of depth perception, Geck missed. He only brushed against the green-skinned cook and instead careened into the live aquariums, which the Mage chef had opened, preparatory to serving. Both glass cases toppled over, dumping out a menagerie of edible horrors. Hundreds of mutated crawdads and assorted live tentacles went thrashing into the crowd. People began screaming.

McGoo yelled, "Watch out! The ingredients are loose."

Tentacles flung themselves on fleeing mummies. Crawfish clipped their pincers on the spiky fur of a punk rocker werewolf, who clawed his own cheeks in an attempt to get them off.

The Kitchen Litch quickly evacuated from the grandstand, taking the last samples of fricasseed beetles with her, but in her alarm, she bumped the sealed container of frrresh, live, blood-sucking gnats that she had reserved for garnish, and the swarm of black biting things flew up, indiscriminately buzzing around everyone on the stage.

Next to the cauldron, the Cajun Mage flailed, trying to beat back the frenzied one-eyed newt.

Rocky and Ned cleared a way through the crowd with all the finesse of two bulldozers, knocking people aside on their way to the stage. I followed them.

Ned bellowed at the chef in his cavernous voice, "We're going to need that eye back!"

"*I'm* going to need it!" Geck jumped up and down, grabbing for the vial clenched in the Mage's green hand.

More large black beetles had escaped from the Kitchen Litch's wicker basket, and Leatherneck, seemingly unphased by the chaos, reached out with his big strangler's hands and grabbed them to add to his pot of chainsaw chili.

McGoo stomped on the assorted tentacles and kicked away crawdads that nipped at his ankles. "Keep calm!" he yelled.

The golem and the rock monster got themselves so entangled in the rebellious ingredients that I made it to the stage first. The cloud of blood-sucking gnats swarmed around me, but the biting creatures went away disappointed, with no taste for embalming fluid.

The Cajun Mage looked indignantly into his étouffée. "But this would have been the perfect batch. You've ruined everything!" He dodged the newt and opened the glass vial. "Without the secret ingredient, it might as well just be a casserole. I must finish for the sake of the culinary arts!" He upended the vial over the cauldron.

As if in slow motion, Geck groaned, "Nooooo!"

But I got there just in time, lashing out with my

outstretched hand. I caught the detached eye of newt in my palm, and it plopped there, sitting moist and squishy, unpleasant to the touch ... but safe.

Rocky and Ned reached the stage just as I backed away cradling Geck's eye. The golem and the rock monster grabbed the Cajun Mage, lifted him up, and dumped him into the large pot of nightmare étouffée, where he stirred and whisked himself helplessly.

Geck hurried over to me, trembling. "You saved my eye! Do you think it can be reattached?"

"There's a good chance. We have the best mad scientists in the Quarter," I said. "Though, from now on, you may need reading glasses."

Rocky the golem loomed over me. "That'll be five bucks."

"Each," said Ned.

I carefully handed the jiggly eye to Geck's loving care, while I dug in my wallet. By now, most of the crowd had run screaming and the loose ingredients had dispersed.

The Kitchen Litch had run away, plagued by vengeful beetles, and the only one remaining on the stand was burly Leatherneck, who calmly ate his chili straight from the ladle. "Last chef standing. I guess that means I win."

McGoo handcuffed the thoroughly étoufféed Cajun chef, who was still trapped inside his cauldron, although out of courtesy he turned the heat down to a slow simmer. The Ragin' Cajun Mage struggled to lift a gooped finger to his lips, tasted it, "After all that, it still could use salt."

I called Sheyenne back at the office and asked her to look up the best eyeball replacers in the Quarter. I suggested that Gunther the imp might be able to give a recommendation.

Out in the wreckage in front of the grandstand, I saw Albert and two of his waitresses running around with shovels and five-gallon buckets, scooping up the dropped samples of Texas chainsaw chili and fricasseed beetles. I could guess what might be on tomorrow's special board for the Ghoul's Diner.

Leaving McGoo to take care of the arrested chef, I led Geck back toward my offices. I recalled that I had promised to take Sheyenne out for a dinner date, but I realized I didn't have much appetite.

Maybe we would go dancing instead.

Head Case

A t a glance, I could tell that the little conscience demon who came into our offices was the "bad" one—scarlet body shaped like a miniature devil, horns on his forehead, pointed tail, even down to the diminutive pitchfork. Since he was only about as big as my hand, he looked kind of cute (though I wouldn't have told him so, since that was sure to evoke a tantrum).

Sheyenne, my ghost girlfriend and office manager, had cooed and called him "oh, how darling!" which only annoyed the little guy further as he asked to engage the services of Chambeaux & Deyer Investigations. He was hyperactive, easily provoked ... and right now the conscience demon was desperate.

Which was why he'd come to see us in the first place.

"If they can't find a body, there's no crime, right? They can't arrest me or charge me with murder?" The little demon's arrow-pointed tail thrashed back and forth. He wobbled his pointed pitchfork as he pranced on the tabletop in the conference room.

"Careful," I said, "you're going to poke somebody's eye out with that thing."

Across the table sat Robin Deyer, my lovely and talented business partner, the best lawyer to appear since the Big Uneasy returned all of the monsters to the world. Robin looked up from her yellow legal pad. The spell-attached pencil scribbled notes all by itself as fast as she could think of things to record. "But there's a crime if you've just confessed to it, Mr. ... ?"

"Conscience Demon," he said. "CD for short."

"I'm pretty good at digging up bodies," I said. "I'm a zombie of many talents."

The little demon swiveled around on the table. "I'm not interested in you as a zombie, Mr. Shamble, but as a detective."

"It's *Chambeaux*," I said out of habit, though the imp wasn't interested.

"Most importantly," he continued, "I'm here because I need a lawyer. A defense attorney. Can you save my bacon, Ms. Deyer?" He lowered his voice to a sultry, tempting tone. "I really like bacon. You should eat more of it. Don't worry about your cholesterol or your arteries. It tastes so good." Then he shook his head, snapping his attention back to his own urgency. "If there's no body, they can't pin it on me, right? No one will even investigate the crime, right? Why would they bother? No one will miss him. No one could stand him!"

"Just because you can't stand somebody doesn't mean you can murder them," I pointed out.

Robin added, "Dan's right. There's a lot of legal precedent."

The conscience demon grumbled. "He was impossible to live with. Such a goody-two-shoes! Always getting in the way and thinking too much. So, I took that ridiculous halo above his head and strangled him with it. Sometimes you have to do what feels right without thinking about it too much. And, boy, did that feel right!"

"So ... you killed your counterpart demon?" I asked. "The angelic one?"

Robin tapped a finger on her yellow legal pad while the pencil continued taking notes. "Don't answer that, Mr. CD, because it's best if we don't know the answer."

"But you're my lawyer," the little devil said. "You have to defend me! You have to protect me. You're supposed to presume I'm innocent. Besides, don't we have confidentiality? If I can't be honest with my own defense attorney, who can I be honest with?" He scratched his backside with one of the tines of his pitchfork. "And I don't usually make it a practice to be honest."

"I'm not supposed to presume you're innocent," Robin explained. "Once I accept you as a client, then I'm supposed to defend you to the best of my ability. And even once we do have lawyer-client confidentiality, attorneys generally don't ask outright if the client committed a crime."

"But the ends justify the means," CD said.

"That's another common misunderstanding of the law."

Sheyenne's ethereal form drifted in, bringing refreshments, green tea for Robin, sour old coffee for me, and a miniscule cup of water for the imp. His cup was so small I had to look twice before I realized it was the rinsed-out cap from a tube of toothpaste.

"Who defines good and evil?" CD asked. "That's my job, isn't it? Maybe I can be an expert witness in my own trial, right?"

I could tell Robin was getting exasperated. She was in her late twenties with smooth, coffee-colored skin and intense brown eyes. She'd been raised upper middle class, gotten her law degree, and decided to seek justice for the unnaturals because the downtrodden ghosts, mummies, and golems in the Unnatural Quarter needed her help much more than any fat-cat corporate executive did. While it's not a glamourous job, Robin found it satisfying. As far as I could tell she never regretted her late hours or her sometimes frustrating clients.

Before Robin could continue to explain the subtleties of the law, we heard a loud *thump* against the outer wall of the office. Sheyenne's luminous form brightened as she spun in the air. "It's coming from out in the hallway."

"Maybe someone's knocking on our door," I said. If it turned out to be another new client, this was shaping up to be a good month.

The thump came again. "Definitely not the door," Robin said.

Sheyenne flitted out of the conference room, and I followed her, proud of my smooth muscle movement. I'm a well-preserved zombie. I exercise regularly to keep the rigor mortis at bay, I make regular trips to the embalming parlor for a touch-up, and I take care of my physical appearance. Other than being a little gray-skinned and, of course, dead, I'm a good-looking guy. And a decent detective.

We heard the muffled thud one more time, and Sheyenne flitted straight through the door without opening it, which is an advantage of being incorporeal. I opened the door just as I heard shouts coming from one of the other offices here on the building's second floor.

"You clumsy oaf! You're scaring away the customers."

As a P.I., my mind is like a steel trap, and my powers of observation are instantaneous. I immediately noticed several things: First, the small mustachioed and florid-faced man who called himself the Angry Hatter stood in the doorway of his shop down the hall. His hair was curly and unkempt, as if he tried on hats all day long. The Angry Hatter was the proprietor of a new boutique haberdashery, though despite his infuriated shouts I couldn't see any customers that were in danger of being scared away.

Second, I saw a large man wearing a black turtleneck and a dark sports jacket careening down the hall. He was disoriented, losing his balance and repeatedly thumping into the wall.

Third, I noticed the man had no head, which under normal circumstances should have been the primary thing to notice, but here in the Unnatural Quarter there's really no such thing as normal.

Sheyenne drifted down the hall, trying to intercept the headless guy. He didn't seem to know where he was going, but in his hand he held a scrawled and nearly illegible note, waving the paper in front of him. "I've lost my head. Have you seen it?"

Sheyenne drifted close. "Here, sir. Let me help you down the hall. I'll take you into our offices."

Judging from the note, I assumed the poor decapitation victim was looking for us. I lurched forward to intercept him. Always trying to stay friendly with my neighbors in the building, I gave a reassuring wave to the florid-faced Angry Hatter. "We'll take it from here. Sorry for the disturbance."

The haberdasher had tried to drum up business with memorable radio ads that played too often. In his loud, exuberant voice he railed, "I'm not just a *mad* hatter, I'm *angry*! And that lets me give you the best prices!"

Judging from the lack of customers, the ad wasn't very effective.

As a ghost, Sheyenne can't touch any living thing, so she couldn't help guide the headless guy. I took his arm and led him stumbling down the hall to our offices. Robin and the little conscience demon were both there, curious.

I led the new client to Sheyenne's desk, trying to pump him for more information. He held up his piece of paper, giving us the basics of the case, but it wasn't enough for me to start investigating. "You'll have to tell us a little more about yourself, sir," I said.

Sheyenne yanked out the printer tray and removed a sheet of white paper, then placed a pen in the man's hand. "First off, can you tell us your name? Write it out for us?"

Robin watched, curious and concerned. The devilish imp hopped on her shoulder to get a better view, but she quickly brushed him off. CD sat on the corner of Sheyenne's desk instead.

He fumbled with the pen and scrawled across the paper. He misjudged the edge so that the latter part of his letters ran off onto the desk. "HEADLESS GUY."

"Headless Guy?" I asked. "That's your name?"

The big man shook his shoulders, and I realized that he was trying to nod but without a head. "That's a very appropriate name," Sheyenne said.

Guy tried to write more, but his letters were ill-formed and crossed over his other words, then ran off the paper. He scribbled so fast we couldn't read any of it, but he seemed full of things to say.

"I have an idea," I said. "Can you type?"

When Headless Guy's shoulder bobbed again, apparently another nod, I set him down in Sheyenne's office chair and placed his hands on her keyboard. He immediately began to type, frantic to explain himself. Good thing he didn't need to hunt and peck. If you're a man without a head, it's imperative you learn to be a touch typist.

Unfortunately, only a mishmash of garbled letters appeared on the screen, until I realized that his fingers were offset. So I adjusted his hands, made sure his fingers were in home position, then Headless Guy began to type again.

"I've lost my head. It's gone! I've been looking everywhere. Can you help me find it?"

The little imp sprang from the corner of the desk and landed on Headless Guy's shoulder. "How can you look for anything when you don't have a head?"

Guy shrugged, making CD bounce up and down.

Sounding compassionate, Sheyenne said, "At least he found his way here to us, and we can help him."

"I always appreciate resourceful clients," I said. He must have heard of my skills as a detective. "When was the last time you saw your head?"

Headless Guy pondered, then began to type out in detail. "It was just another lazy Sunday. We went for a walk, so my head could smell the flowers around the drainage ditches. We went to the candy store because my head likes hard candies. He used to like drinking coffee, but that's a mess unless I adjust him carefully over my neck. Then we went hat shopping because my head is very fond of hats. Then we went to hear a skeleton jazz band, because my head likes music, even though I can't hear. And I don't like jazz anyway ... but you have to be patient with your partner. We've been together so long."

I frowned. "You mean your head and your body?"

Ignoring my question, Guy kept typing. "When I woke up, my head was gone. I'm sure it's been kidnapped! Someone's holding my head for ransom, but I haven't found a ransom note yet." With his big hands, he patted his jacket, fumbled in his pockets, then went back to typing, somehow finding the right position on the keyboard again. "What am I going to do? I'm lost without my head. Can you help me, Mr. Shamble?"

Even typing, he spelled my name wrong ... but I don't hold that against a potential client.

"Maybe somebody buried it," the conscience demon

suggested, still perched on Headless Guy's shoulder. "And you'll never find the body. It worked for me."

"You're not helping, CD," I pointed out.

"We have the body right here," Robin said. "And we'll help you find your head."

"First, the formalities," I said, already formulating my plan. The cases don't solve themselves. "We better go down to the police station and talk with Officer McGoohan. We'll file a missing person's report." I reconsidered. "Or a missing *piece* of a person report."

Headless Guy stood from the office chair, eager to follow me, but he crashed into the desk. Recovering himself, Guy moved in the other direction and lurched into the chair, nearly tripping.

Exasperated, CD kept his balance on the dark jacketed shoulder. "This is ridiculous! Let me help you out, right?" The devilish little creature broke into a wide, malicious grin. "I won't steer you wrong."

Officer Toby McGoohan, or "McGoo" to his friends, is a wisecracking, insensitive but reasonably confident beat cop who was no more happy about his transfer to the Unnatural Quarter than his superiors were to hear his offensive and politically incorrect ethnic jokes, which had led to the transfer in the first place. Here among the monsters, McGoo could be as rude as he liked since unnaturals had thick skins … sometimes scaly skins, sometimes covered in spines or fur.

I led Headless Guy through the bustle of the UQPD. I made my way past the ringing phones, the officers typing on keyboards, other cops dragging a wide variety of hand-cuffed perps. McGoo's desk was in back, and I waved at some of the other cops. They were all familiar with the most prominent undead detective in the Quarter.

The imp on Headless Guy's shoulder directed him. "Straight forward, two more steps, now a little to your left." Guy crashed his hip into the corner of a detective's desk, scattering the papers from an inbox. "Sorry, I meant *right*, not left," CD said.

Headless Guy stumbled along, bumped into another desk, and I realized that the imp was teasing him. That made me impatient. "Come on. Let's go. This is serious business."

"Yes, but it's fun too, right?" said CD. But he did cease his practical jokes, and we arrived at McGoo's desk.

"Hey Shamble," he said, looking at Guy. "Let me guess, he's a jogger who doesn't remember to duck when he runs under low bridges? Or maybe it was a low-flying haircut?"

The conscience demon snickered. "I like him! For a cop."

"We're not here to talk about how Headless Guy lost his head in the first place," I said. "We're more interested in the *second* time he lost his head, and it was recent. We think his head has been kidnapped and is being held for ransom."

McGoo took out a set of forms. "Sorry to hear that, Mr. Guy." His serious tone lasted only a moment before he turned to me. "Sounds like you've got a real *head case* here, Shamble."

McGoo has freckled skin, reddish hair, and a wide mouth with a persistent grin that made him always seem to get in trouble. In our work in the Unnatural Quarter, I often got McGoo into trouble, and he did the same for me. He's my BHF, my Best Human Friend, and that's what friends are for.

"We've come to fill out a missing person's report," I said. "And then I'll start investigating."

McGoo scribbled some information on the form, looked at Headless Guy, then tore off the bottom third. "It's just a partial missing person's form, for just a partial missing person."

"The joke's already been made, McGoo," I said, and he seemed disappointed.

"Give me a description of your head," he said. "We'll need to be able to identify it."

The conscience demon on his shoulder peered down into the open mouth of the turtleneck but didn't hear any answer.

"He's better off using your keyboard, McGoo," I said.

Headless Guy typed out descriptions. The height of the head, the color of hair (brown), wavy locks (well-combed), eye color (beautiful, hauntingly blue), distinguishing features (chiseled nose, square jaw, handsome features, a perfect smile).

McGoo snorted. "Sounds like he's describing me."

"I don't think he'd want your head as replacement, McGoo."

"We'll put out an all-points bulletin to see if anyone spots a suspicious looking head."

Agitated, Headless Guy typed on the keyboard using all caps to show his exasperation. "IT'S BEEN KIDNAPPED!"

"We better go find the ransom note," I suggested. "Once we've made contact with the headnappers, then your missing head will have a lot more to stand on."

McGoo got right to work, after his coffee break.

After we finished, the conscience demon began whispering down into the turtleneck. "It's not so bad really. Think of your options now! You're free to do what you want for the first time in your life. Effectively you're a bachelor. Live a little, right?"

Headless Guy did not seem overly enthusiastic, although I couldn't read his expression. He followed me, occasionally bumping into desks and people as we left the police station. CD worked harder at giving him better guidance.

If Headless Guy's head had been kidnapped from his apartment, then that was the obvious first place to look for clues. The scene of the crime—it was in Chapter One of every detective's handbook.

Headless Guy followed me with CD on his shoulders providing mostly helpful directions, making sure he didn't bump into too many obstacles on the way. Guy looked dapper in his black turtleneck and dark jacket, but he wasn't much of a conversationalist.

In the companionable silence, I mulled over possibilities, using him as a (silent) sounding board as we climbed the stairs to his third-floor apartment in a rent-controlled complex for unnaturals of modest means. If the head had been kidnapped, then why would anyone want it? Obviously, Guy was not a wealthy man, so he could never afford a large ransom. I had forgotten to ask him what he, or his head, did for a living, and maybe that was relevant. Was it for blackmail? Did the head possess any special, valuable, or dangerous knowledge? Had the head witnessed a terrible crime, perhaps? Something so awful he hadn't dared tell his body?

Or maybe the head was an accountant helping to launder money in illicit operations. If so, the head might have many important facts and figures in his memory. The head might be held hostage.

Headless Guy wasn't saying. His empty turtleneck didn't speak a word.

We reached the door at the end of a dimly lit hall. Loud, thrumming music came from the next-door neighbors. Shrieking banshee children howled as they played and wrestled, and even the muffled noise was loud enough to crack glass.

"We're here," CD said, bouncing up and down on Headless Guy's shoulder. "Get out your key. We'll find the ransom note in there."

"We don't know what we'll find, but we should be

prepared." I reached into the pocket of my sport jacket, making sure I carried my .38 for protection, though I preferred to use harsh language, unless a situation got really extreme.

Guy fumbled in the left pocket of his trousers and pulled out a keyring, trying to find the right one by feel. But he couldn't accurately hit the keyhole, so he dropped the chain to the floor. He bent over and fumbled around, but I quickly snatched the keys and unlocked the door, which swung open with a creak on old hinges.

I could sense a tension in the air, and I cautiously entered the dim apartment. No lights were on, but then I didn't suppose Headless Guy had much use for lamps. Maybe I should have brought McGoo along, or even Sheyenne because a ghost could scout ahead by passing through walls.

"Hello! Anybody here?" the feisty imp called, startling me.

"So much for our element of surprise," I said.

"Ah, but that was unpredictable, right?" asked CD. "It's good to be unpredictable." I didn't argue the point.

We heard no sound from within, and I entered, doing a quick assessment, especially trying to spot any signs of a struggle—overturned furniture, ransacked drawers, smashed lamps. But no, Headless Guy's apartment looked comfortable, just like any other place set up for a man with no head, and a head with discriminating taste in interior decorating. A sofa, a kitchenette table, a television set, a coffee table, an end table, bookshelves, and a small stand for propping up a book adjacent to a pedestal where presumably the head would be propped when it wanted to read.

And hats, a great many hats, arrayed on a separate set of shelves, hung on a hat stand near the corner, dangling from pegs on the wall. Dapper top hats, porkpies, bowlers, numerous baseball caps with sports team logos, even a colorful propeller beanie, apparently for when the head felt facetious.

"Your head really enjoyed stylish hats," I said. "There must be one here for every day of the month."

When Headless Guy didn't respond, the conscience demon leaned over and shouted down into the empty hole of the turtleneck. "He said it looks like your head really likes hats!"

Seeming dejected, Guy let his shoulders slump. He walked through the apartment easily navigating the hazards of furniture, not bumping into any table corners or chairs. He made his way over to the bed up against one wall and sagged down on the creaking mattress. He sat dejected and leaned forward, putting the empty space where his head would have been into his hands.

CD shook his head, waving his little pitchfork. "Man, this Guy is miserable."

Still looking for the ransom note, I circled the shelves, poked at the hats in their hat boxes or hooks, even picked up the propeller beanie and spun it in my fingers. I went into the kitchen, where several dishes had been washed and stacked in the sink. The small kitchenette table had one chair for Guy to sit, and a little stand for his head so the two could have dinner together.

I found the note in the middle of the table lying in plain sight. Anyone with a head, or at least eyes, would have seen it right away.

"This is it!" I grabbed the paper.

"The ransom note?" asked CD.

Guy lurched to his feet and stumbled into the kitchen. I read the note, expecting to find threats and terms, dollar amounts, secret instructions … but it wasn't that at all. This letter was devastating in a completely different way.

"It's a Dear John letter."

"His name is Guy, not John," said the conscience demon.

I cleared my throat, because that seemed to be an appropriate thing to do, and read the words out loud, not sure whether Headless Guy could hear me.

"'Guy, I'm sorry but the time has come. I'm leaving you. I just can't keep sticking out my neck for you anymore.'" I swallowed hard. Guy stood stiff as a tree, stunned. But my client deserved to have all the answers.

I continued, "'You're boring, sluggish, lethargic, and a terrible conversationalist. You never want to have fun. You don't stimulate my intellect.'" I swallowed hard and muttered apologetically, "Sorry, that's what the words say."

Guy's shoulders slumped even further, knocking the conscience demon off balance, but he jammed his tiny pitchfork into the fabric of the jacket and held on.

"'I've found someone else, someone who shares my passions. I'm going to the Angry Hatter, a man who appreciates me for what I am. Don't try to change my mind. This is the only way I can get ahead in life.'"

Headless Guy collapsed onto the lone chair by the kitchen table. His body shuddered, wracked with unexpressed sobs.

"It's not the answer you wanted, but at least your head is safe," I said. "This isn't over yet. Let's go talk with him."

Headless Guy couldn't move on with his life until at least he faced his faithless head, but I knew that domestic disputes and inflamed passions rarely turned out well. Solving a kidnapping might have been easier.

Although I'm a crack private investigator and very good at what I do, sometimes I'm a clumsy oaf when it comes to delicate emotional matters. Both Sheyenne and Robin have told me that enough times, so I take them at their word, even though I've personally seen no evidence of tactlessness. Who was I to say? The bullet hole in the middle of my forehead is clear evidence that I don't always get along with people.

Returning to our building with Headless Guy and the conscience demon riding on his shoulder, somewhat subdued now, I decided not to go straight to the Angry Hatter's haberdashery. I needed to bring out the big guns, the emotional and relationship experts. I wanted Robin and Sheyenne there as moral and emotional support—and to help me pull my foot out of my mouth if I happened to say the wrong thing.

With a stern-looking Robin on my left and Headless Guy on my right, I marched down the hall from our offices. Sheyenne drifted ahead of us, her luminous form glowing with anger. She was indignant on Guy's behalf, although I knew that painful breakups usually had two sides to the story.

As we converged on the Angry Hatter's shop with shades drawn and the door closed, the haberdashery seemed to willfully disinvite customers. Sheyenne forgot herself and pounded on the door, but her ghostly hand simply slipped through without making a noise. Then she concentrated on her poltergeist abilities and knocked more successfully.

Since it was during normal business hours, I didn't feel we had to knock. "Let's surprise them. Better to keep them off-balance."

We all entered a hat shop that was filled with countless colorful hats, women's fashions, gaudy Easter bonnets, and spring flowers. Gentlemen's hats were lovingly arranged on another shelf. The air smelled of simmering potpourri.

At a little table in the middle of the shop, the Angry Hatter sat holding a china cup with a teapot in front of him. Across the table, a disembodied head sat on an ornate brass stand. A china cup of tea was close enough to the mouth that the head could drink through a properly positioned straw. The head wore a gaudy, frilly, lavender spring hat adorned with ribbons and fake flowers, like something Queen Elizabeth II might have worn on one of her more hallucinogenic days.

Startled by our abrupt entry, Guy's Head spat out the straw and sputtered his tea. I saw a little dribble of hot liquid run out the bottom of his neck into a catch basin beneath the stand, thereby solving the inconvenience of a head drinking tea without an attached body.

The Angry Hatter lunged to his feet, his face florid, his long mustache sticking out like a sharp weapon on each side. He blurted out the standard line of all guilty persons caught in the act. "What is the meaning of this?"

"It's about time you found my note," Guy's Head sneered.

Headless Guy lumbered forward, raised both hands in a beseeching gesture.

"We found it all right," I said. "He hired Chambeaux & Deyer, and we always solve our cases."

"Well, I did leave the note right out on the table," said Guy's Head. "It couldn't have been too much of a challenge."

The Angry Hatter stood fuming, balling his fists. Though he was barely five feet tall, he could swing a roundhouse punch and strike Headless Guy directly in the crotch. Even though he was missing everything from his shoulders on up, I assumed Guy was fully equipped down there in his second male brain.

"You have no business here!" said the hatter.

"How do you know we're not customers?" I asked. "I was thinking of buying a propeller beanie for myself."

Robin said in a stern voice, "You put our client through a great deal of emotional pain and suffering."

"Breakups happen," said Guy's Head, not sounding at all apologetic.

Sheyenne looked soulful as she opened wide her beautiful blue eyes. "How could you hurt the poor Guy like that? Why don't you two try going to counseling?"

"Because I don't want counseling!" snapped Guy's Head. "I want a better partner."

The fuming haberdasher stomped around to the other side of the tea table and gently removed the ridiculous lavender hat so he could stroke the wavy hair on Guy's Head. "We're a perfect match, and don't you try to convince us otherwise! Don't make me angry. You wouldn't like me when I'm angry."

"I don't like you right now," I said.

Headless Guy waved his hands, gesturing plaintively. He placed his palms together in a prayerful gesture, but Guy's Head merely sniffed.

On his shoulder, the conscience demon harrumphed. "That head doesn't deserve you, Guy. You're better off without it. Think of how much fun we could have, just you and me, right? I got your back."

The head struggled, somehow managed to swivel itself about an inch to the left so he could look directly at Robin. "I demand a legal separation."

Robin's expression was hard. "In this particular case, it's called a legal decapitation." She gave an apologetic look to Headless Guy, who couldn't see her anyway. "And I'm afraid one party can request it. Your head is within his rights."

Still stroking the wavy hair, the Angry Hatter turned

the head to one side so he no longer needed to look at his forlorn former body.

CD was having none of it. "I promise I'll show you great fun. I won't steer you wrong. We'll have a good time, and you'll never once regret that cheating head, right? Just look at the Angry Hatter. He's one argument away from a blood pressure stroke, and then what's your head going to do? Come crawling back? No way—it's just you and me now."

Headless Guy squared his shoulders, drawing his resolve.

Suddenly, on his opposite shoulder a bright glow appeared in the air and a white angelic figure formed—another conscience demon, this one sporting stubby little wings and a tiny gold halo that hovered above the blond locks of its head. The angelic conscience demon gave a beautiful smile. "We'll both guide you. We'll provide you with the balance and the happiness you need in your life."

"What the hell are you doing here?" CD demanded, waving his tiny pitchfork. "I strangled you! I got rid of you for good."

"Then why aren't you in jail?" asked the angelic conscience demon in a voice of beatific calm.

"Because there wasn't a body and nobody could pin the crime on me!"

"Even though he blabs it to anyone within earshot," Robin said with a sigh.

The angelic imp smiled. "And there you are, my friend. You can't keep a good man down, and I am definitely, completely good. I was just taking time to meditate, and now I've manifested myself again. You need me, and Headless Guy needs both of us."

I looked at the two opposing conscience demons and said to Robin. "I guess we don't need to defend CD against murder charges now. He didn't really kill his partner."

"I did! I know I did!" CD stomped his little hooves on Headless Guy's shoulder, but Guy reached up to put a hand on each shoulder, gently tapping the two conscience demons as if to reassure them.

"I think we're done here," I said. "Case closed. There's nothing more we can do. Domestic disputes never end with anyone satisfied." I turned to the Angry Hatter. "I'll get my propeller beanie from a different store. Although those fedoras do look nice ..."

"I'll do the separation paperwork," Robin said, resigned, "though it's not the happy ending I would have hoped for."

"It's a happy ending for us," said Guy's Head with a sniff.

The Angry Hatter selected a pale-yellow hat with a wide floppy brim and dangling ribbons. He placed it on the head. "We'll have so much fun together."

Guy lurched out of the haberdashery, gathering his pride as he walked away with the two conscience demons giving him directions.

As we left the haberdashery and headed back to our offices, Sheyenne slipped her spectral hand into my undead one. "Not everyone can have a relationship as perfect as ours, Beaux."

I thought of our times together, how she'd been

poisoned to death after we first started dating and then came back as a ghost ... and then I was shot in the head while investigating her murder. But we still had each other.

"Not everyone can be as perfect as us, Spooky," I agreed, and we went back to work on our more solvable cases.

High Midnight

Gunfire rang out in the Unnatural Quarter—one loud shot, then five more in quick succession.

The audience, both humans and monsters, applauded and whistled. The ghost of the Old West gunslinger, Deadeye One-Eye, had nailed all six target playing cards that hung by clothespins on a wire, right through the Ace of Spades. He shifted his eyepatch in triumph; depth perception did not seem to be necessary for his aim.

"Golly!" said Mild Bill, twirling his spectral handlebar mustache. "And he was only listed as a mid-range gunslinger ghost." He stood with a bowlegged stance, putting his hands on his spectral hips as if he imagined holsters there.

"All right, I'm impressed," I said, standing next to him at the edge of the performance area in the fake western town erected for the show. I couldn't shoot that well with my .38—not when I was alive, and not now that I'm undead. As a zombie detective I might be stiffer, but that didn't mean my aim was steadier.

While the spectators continued to cheer, the ghost of the outlaw gunslinger twirled his pearl-handled ghost Colt revolver and slid it into a shimmering translucent holster. Maybe intangible firearms were easier to twirl than real ones.

Since it was the weekend and late in the evening, I took time off from Chambeaux & Deyer Investigations so we could go see Mild Bill's Wild West Show, an extravagant, if kitschy, affair that the ghost saloon owner had sponsored. And since Robin Deyer, my human lawyer partner, had worked with Mild Bill to take care of all the necessary contracts and waivers, she insisted that attending the show was part of our job. Half the population of the Unnatural Quarter had decided to come out as well.

"It's bound to be a financial success, Beaux," said Sheyenne, my ghost girlfriend, as she intangibly snuggled up to me. "The Wild West show could become a regular thing in the Quarter."

"Why yes, Miss Sheyenne," I said in a long drawl and tipped my fedora as if it were a cowboy hat, sliding it down to cover the bullet hole in the center of my forehead, from where I'd been killed a few years back.

I'd been a reasonably successful human detective in the Unnatural Quarter, solving the usual run of oddball and mundane cases for the humans and monsters that lived there. After I was killed on a case and then rose from the grave—thereby changing my job title from human detective to zombie detective—business had really picked up.

The Wild West show continued. Deadeye One-Eye took a break to reload his six-shooter with ghost bullets, and the dance hall girls came out—vampire girls from the Full Moon Brothel. The ladies of the night (but weren't all vampire women ladies of the night?) enjoyed dressing up in flouncy old-fashioned Western dresses. A female were-wolf capped each side of the line, and they bounced out kicking and stepping high in an untrained version of the can-can—which I wasn't sure was historically accurate … but what do I know? My knowledge of the Old West came from TV reruns, and mid-twentieth century television programming wasn't known for its veracity.

"Whoo hoo, go dance hall girls!" shouted McGoo—Officer Toby McGoohan, my Best Human Friend. As a beat cop, he had been transferred from a human precinct for telling non-politically correct jokes. We helped each other out on cases.

I was surprised by his enthusiastic wolf whistles. "You never showed any interest in the Full Moon ladies before, McGoo."

"Still no interest," he said. "I have enough trouble with human women. I don't need to get involved with Unnaturals."

Robin frowned skeptically at him. "You have trouble with human women? I've never heard you talk about even getting a date."

A flush suffused his freckled face. "And that is exactly my trouble."

After the dance hall girls exited the stage, a troop of ghost cowboys galloped out on wild and unruly nightmares, fiery-eyed black horses that looked frightening and difficult to control, but the ghost riders rode bareback as they twirled lariats over their heads.

Someone had loosed a minotaur into the performance area, and the big bull-headed creature stumbled around with a look of abject confusion. When the ghost cowboys thundered toward the minotaur, he bleated and huffed in alarm. They twirled their ropes and dropped the lassoes around him, cinched him tight, and tied him up, ankles and wrists. The minotaur crashed to the dusty performance ground—again, to much applause.

The minotaur bellowed, "I was just looking for the concession stand."

Next to us, the ghost of Mild Bill let out a belly laugh. "Yesirree, you never can guess what might happen at one of my shows. Lordy!" When he grinned, he showed off bad, brown teeth from chewing ghost tobacco.

Mild Bill owned the New Deadwood Saloon, which had been decorated like an Old West watering hole. He claimed to be the actual ghost of Wild Bill Hickok, but he had mellowed with age, and now he preferred to be called Mild Bill.

Enthusiastic about his Wild West Show, Bill had rented a cursed Indian burial ground for the venue and hired Robin to work out the real estate paperwork and the lease. During negotiations, Robin discovered that the owners could not prove that the burial ground had any legitimate curses, and therefore could not charge extra, so Mild Bill had gotten a reduced rate.

Our Robin always insists that Unnaturals are treated fairly under the law.

After the roped-up minotaur was dragged away from the field, Deadeye One-Eye came back into the middle of the wide dirt main street, twirled his Colt again, and started shooting cigars from the mouths of two volunteer mummies, who trembled as the ends of the stogies were blasted into fragments. Sheyenne, Robin, and McGoo joined in the cheers.

The gunslinger fired his pistols into the air. "And that's just a warm-up for tonight's late show, folks." He had a sinister undertone in his voice. "If y'all think I'm good, wait 'til the rest of my gang comes at high midnight. Moondance McClantock and the boys can shoot circles around me—if they're feeling their oats, they can even shoot triangles." The audience applauded as he sauntered away.

Finished with his act, the ghost of Deadeye One-Eye came up to where we were standing at the edge of the performance field. Even with his eyepatch, his eyesight couldn't be as bad as his teeth. Despite his unfortunate dental condition, he wasn't shy about showing off his smile. The ghost gunslinger tipped his hat at Sheyenne and Robin, then he fixed his single eye on me. "Dan Chambeaux, Zombie Detective." Somehow, he made my name into a sneer.

I acted professional. "I'm surprised you pronounced my name correctly. Most people call me Shamble."

"I know who you are, Chambeaux—but maybe you don't." He showed off his preposterous teeth in a snaggly snarl rather than a grin. "Are you aware your great-great umpty-ump grandpappy, Dirk Chambeaux, was a hated marshal in these parts, give or take a state or two? He was a feared man, made a lot of enemies."

McGoo nudged me with an elbow. "Hey Shamble, law enforcement is in your blood."

"My blood these days is embalming fluid," I said.

Deadeye One-Eye gave me a careful assessment before striding off. "See you later tonight—at high midnight."

"What did he mean by that?" Robin asked.

"No idea."

During the preparations for the Wild West show, I had watched Robin go through excruciating negotiations and legal convolutions. The ghosts of the McClantock outlaw gang had a ruthless talent representative, and affable Mild Bill was a babe in the woods when it came to making a deal with a cutthroat agent—literally a cutthroat, because he was an accused serial killer, although it was never proven. The agent claimed the gunslinger ghosts were in high demand and tried to extract an outrageous appearance fee. Deadeye One-Eye, though, was a free agent, and he had quickly come to terms for a far lower fee, for which he had been resoundingly criticized by his gang because his concession had affected their collective bargaining power.

Mild Bill wanted to book the McClantock gang for multiple performances, along with roving freelance entertainment—gun tricks and such among the crowd—but the cutthroat agent had tried to triple their fee. At one point, Robin had been so frustrated that I lurched into the negotiating room to ask if she needed any muscle to bring the gunslingers in line. It was a joke (zombies aren't really all that intimidating), but when the agent went back to Moondance McClantock, they promptly agreed to the high midnight show.

I guess I was more scary than I thought.

But Mild Bill could only afford the one designated performance, explicitly defined as a single round of extravagant gun play, nothing else. Any more would be a breach of contract. Despite his disappointment, Mild Bill had promised to make the best of it.

Around the show grounds, the spectral saloon owner put up posters featuring the outlaws. "Wanted: Dead, Undead, or Alive. Moondance McClantock and his gang!" Robin had brought along her executed copy of the contract, just in case McClantock decided to renege on the deal.

Obviously, we all had to stay and see the big performance, which would take place in an hour.

A skeleton played happy piano music in front of the temporary saloon and watering hole, where a potbellied zombie barkeep was pouring beer, whiskey, and shots of blood to cowboy-dressed vampires who looked as if they had just escaped from an undead dude ranch. Albert Gould, the rotting and disheveled proprietor of the Ghoul's Diner, had set up a food stand that served "authentic western barbecue"—blackened bones (species unknown) covered with sizzling meat. I had heard his special sauce was good.

The Old West must have been a peaceful, nostalgic place.

But then, gunfire rang out—real gunfire, in earnest this time, and Deadeye One-Eye was not just aiming at targets. Over by the rickety corral, he had untied the five angry nightmares, and now he whooped like a Hollywood Indian on the warpath. He fired his pistols again and again, and the noise startled the demon horses. Even though they were supernatural creatures, they certainly spooked easily.

The ghost gunslinger laughed maniacally, something he did quite well, and the snorting black horses thundered out in violent panic, racing into the crowd of naturals and unnaturals along the main street.

"Shoot, that's not part of the show!" Mild Bill flashed a glance at Robin. "You said we couldn't afford the insurance for a full stampede."

"We better get these people out of here," I shouted. "And bring the horses under control."

As I lurched into motion, McGoo kept up with me. "Great idea, Shamble. Throw ourselves in front of a bunch of demonic stallions?"

"Don't make it worse than it is, McGoo—these are mares, not stallions."

The horses stormed forward, their hooves striking improbable sparks on the dusty ground. Flames chuffed from their nostrils.

McGoo drew his two service revolvers, one loaded with normal bullets, the other with silver bullets, but I didn't think wild horses would be cowed, regardless the type of ammunition.

As the crowd of mummies, vampires, werewolves, mad scientists, and their assistants fled to the boardwalk and the store fronts, the horses stormed toward us. McGoo opened fire, shooting into the air. If the demonic horses could be spooked once, they could be spooked again.

The resounding gunfire scared the nightmares enough that instead of charging into the crowd, they split up and galloped toward the concession stands. The skeleton piano player and Albert the ghoul fled. The rampaging nightmares crashed into the barbecue display, knocking the tent down and spilling meat-covered bones in all directions, along with a bucket of smoking sauce. The "secret ingredient" burned craters in the sawdust-strewn ground.

Two of the black horses were still coming toward us, and I drew my .38, also firing into the night sky, but my gun wasn't as loud as McGoo's heavier-caliber weapons. I added some harsh language, and that did the trick. The snorting nightmares wheeled about and stampeded back toward their corral.

Then amidst the gunfire and whinnying, I heard something that made my artificial blood run cold—a scream. Sheyenne's scream.

"McGoo, come on," I yelled.

The ghost of the evil gunslinger stood in front of Sheyenne, Robin, and Mild Bill. Deadeye One-Eye had both of his Colts out, and he opened fire. Sheyenne spun, crying out in pain—pain!—as a ghost bullet grazed her upper arm, and I saw a splash of ectoplasmic blood.

Robin was in the line of fire too, but she dove out of the way. Somehow, the bullets missed her.

McGoo and I put on a surge of speed.

The one-eyed ghost gunslinger turned the firepower on his real target, Mild Bill. The avuncular saloon owner raised his hands in surrender. "Don't shoot!"

"Why not?" Deadeye One-Eye emptied his pistols.

Ectoplasmic blood sprayed out from deadly wounds in the ghost saloon owner's chest, like the sauce from a spaghetti western. The ghost gunslinger laughed at what he had done.

McGoo and I ran up, our guns drawn. I had eyes only for Sheyenne, who was wounded, and Mild Bill, who was mortally wounded—for a second time.

In a rage, McGoo snarled, "You are under arrest, Deadeye One-Eye!"

"You'll never take me alive, lawman—it's already too late." The gunslinger sneered at the dying ghost of Mild Bill, then looked up at me. "Now there's no way he can rescind the contract. When Moondance gets here, Chambeaux, you're a dead man."

"I'm pretty sure that's how I started out the day," I said.

The gunslinger's ghost vanished into thin air while he was still laughing.

While McGoo and Robin went to Mild Bill, I raced to Sheyenne. She had clamped a hand against the ghost bullet wound in her shoulder, and red ectoplasmic blood seeped around her fingers.

"How could you get hurt?" I asked. "You're not even corporeal."

"That gunslinger has ghost bullets," Sheyenne said. "And I'm a ghost."

She lifted up her hand, stared at the ectoplasmic blood, and shook her head. She looked beautiful with her blond hair and her startling blue eyes. "I'll be fine Beaux—it's just a flesh wound ... figuratively speaking of course."

McGoo checked over Robin quickly. "You're not hurt?"

"Just lucky, I guess." She looked shocked.

The ghost of Mild Bill lay on the ground, moaning, and his blood evaporated into the spirit world. "Never thought they'd shoot me!" With his dying gaze, he looked up at me and uttered a final sentence. "Shamble ... beware, high midnight." He gasped, let out a death rattle, and his ghost dissipated before our eyes, along with all the bloodstains.

I felt angry and sickened. "Deadeye One-Eye caused the stampede as a diversion. We should've stayed with you three."

"Beaux, you couldn't have known," Sheyenne said.

The nightmares had wandered back to the corral and now munched contentedly on thistles. Several werewolves and zombies had darted into the wreckage of Albert the ghoul's barbecue tent and slunk off with dripping bones, leaving a trail of barbecue sauce that exuded curls of green acidic smoke.

McGoo wiped sweat from his brow. "What did Mild Bill mean about high midnight?"

"That's when the ghosts of the McClantock gang are coming, per the contract," Robin said. "Deadeye One-Eye didn't want Mild Bill to rescind the agreement. He's the only one with a legal signature on it."

Sheyenne tore a strip of gingham from her ectoplasmic dress and tied it around her wound. "It all changed when Dan found out his ancestor was a ruthless Old West lawman."

"But I never heard of Dirk Chambeaux before," I said. "What difference would that make to me?"

Then, on the ground before us where Mild Bill's ghost had died, the air shimmered, flickered, and a second even wispier form of the spectral saloon owner rose up. He seemed even less substantial than before.

"Mild Bill, you're alive!" McGoo said.

"Golly … not hardly. I'm a ghost. But this time I'm a ghost of a ghost."

"What are the chances of that happening?" I asked.

"Pretty damn slim. I wish I'd had this kind of luck when I was alive, yesirree." Mild Bill stroked his handlebar mustache, as if he was particularly pleased with his renewed existence.

Robin asked, "What's going to happen at high midnight? Why should we beware?"

The doubly spectral cowboy blinked at her. "Haven't you been paying attention, Ms. Deyer? Moondance McClantock and his gang are coming back—we arranged for it, you and me. It was all part of their plan. What they really want is to get revenge. Dan's great-great umpty-ump ancestor was Marshal Dirk Chambeaux, the lawman who sent McClantock and his gang to the gallows. They're not just here to perform in my Wild West show, they're coming to get revenge on you." The wispy ghost's mouth drooped in a sincere frown. "And you're going to have to face them at high midnight, Marshal."

"Private investigator," I corrected him. "McGoo's closer to being a marshal."

"Hell, I haven't even made detective yet," McGoo said.

A crowd had begun to gather, listening to the conversation, but when they learned that the murderous gunslingers were coming soon, they backed off, not wanting to be anywhere close to the line of fire. A full-furred werewolf muttered that he had left the bathtub running and quickly retreated. The rest of the crowd eased away with similar, or more outrageous, excuses.

I looked at them all, seeing fear in their eyes. Many of these were clients of mine, past clients and future clients. I stood my ground, turning to face them. "What time is it now?"

The ghost of the ghost of Mild Bill flipped open a pocket watch that hung from a chain in his vest. "Eleven forty-five—fifteen minutes till doomsday."

"Fifteen minutes?" McGoo cried. "Shouldn't there be more time to build up suspense?"

"It's a faster-paced society nowadays, McGoo," I said.

He lifted his chin. "Well, I'm standing with you, Shamble. Something doesn't smell right around here, and it's not just you."

"Thanks, McGoo."

Sheyenne looked weak and dizzy from the ghost gunshot, as if she'd lost some of her spirit, literally. "We'll stay here to help you, Beaux."

"Not you, Spooky—you've already been hurt," I said as

firmly as I could. "If the ghost bullets are flying, I couldn't bear to lose you again. We've got plenty of people around here to help stand against those gunslingers."

I turned to the crowd that McGoo and I had just saved from stampeding demonic horses. Oddly, the spectators that had previously been so numerous now muttered excuses and began to melt away like vampires on a hot summer day.

Even the ghost of Mild Bill's ghost muttered, "I better go check on my saloon. All these frightened people are going to need drinks."

I felt discouraged. "You too?"

"I have already been shot to death once today." He vanished.

I couldn't hold it against him.

McGoo calmly reloaded both of his service revolvers, regular bullets and silver bullets. "I know you would've taken a bullet for me, Shamble."

"As I recall, I already have. What are friends for?" I stood next to him in the middle of the dirt main street, which was bounded on either side by the colorful, but thin, facades of a movie set cowboy town.

The town clock tower, which had been erected for the Wild West show, rang out, sounding 11:55.

"That's an odd time for the hour to chime."

"I think it's to give people time to prepare for the midnight festivities," Sheyenne said.

When the loud bells ceased chiming, the dirt main street on the old cursed burial ground was deserted, dust blowing in the night wind. On either side, the windows were dark in the tall clapboard storefronts, the buildings seemingly abandoned. Back in the corral, the nightmares neighed. The dude ranch vampires had fled, but not too far. I could see them behind the display window of the general store, watching me.

Sheyenne, looking weak and ghostly, drifted to the safety of the boardwalk at my insistence. "Be careful, Beaux—I love you."

"I love you too, Spooky," I said.

Clearly angry, Robin refused to leave us. "This is not the way one should solve problems. We have a legal system, courts, and judges."

"It was the courts and the marshal that ticked off these gunslingers in the first place, Robin," I said.

At precisely 11:57, Moondance McClantock and his gang of murderous gunslinger ghosts appeared, including Deadeye One-Eye, who had joined the party, even though he was a free agent.

McGoo and I faced the six gunslingers in the middle of the main street. The ghost outlaws were a surly, rumpled-looking lot, greasy with sweat and prickly with razor stubble—apparently, none of the spectral gunslingers had found time to bathe or shave in the century and a half since their demise.

"We're here for Chambeaux." Moondance McClantock was a round-faced man with long sideburns, a ten-gallon hat, and enough turquoise and silver to fill an entire roadside souvenir stand. He had a gleaming gold front tooth, which clashed with all the silver and turquoise. "I've waited a long time for this."

"We haven't even met," I said, "and I've only had fifteen minutes to build up my anticipation."

The gang leader shrugged. "Sorry about that. Back in 1856, Marshal Dirk Chambeaux sentenced us all to hang, which wasn't fair."

In unison, the gunslingers all lifted their chins to show off their necks. McClantock shifted a gaudy bolo tie of turquoise and silver to reveal a long rope burn across his throat. The other outlaws had similar noose burns. One man with a full beard and huge eyebrows had a crooked neck as if even his ghost hadn't been able to realign the snapped vertebra.

"A miscarriage of justice," said Deadeye One-Eye.

"Weren't you guilty?" I asked.

"Absolutely," McClantock said. "But my crimes were far worse than any of my boys, here, yet I got the same treatment. I would have gone down in history if he had skinned me alive or burned me over hot coals, but your ancestor lacked imagination, Chambeaux."

"But what does that have to do with me?" I asked.

"We've come here to get our revenge on the last living descendant of Marshal Dirk Chambeaux. You'll pay for his crimes."

I looked at McGoo, then back at the outlaws. "Sorry to point this out, boys, but you missed your chance." I slid back my fedora to reveal the bullet hole in the center of my forehead. "I'm already dead—I'm a zombie. You can't kill me."

I tugged down my sport jacket to show the prominent

stitched-up bullet holes across the chest from yet another time I had been gunned down in the street.

"It'll have to do," McClantock said, and his gunslinger gang members nodded vigorously. "You being dead actually works to our advantage."

"How do you figure?" McGoo asked, fidgeting with his grip on the service revolvers.

"Because we're all ghost gunslingers," Deadeye One-Eye explained. He pulled out both of his Colt pistols; Moondance McClantock did the same, as did all of his boys. "All we have are ghost bullets—and as you saw with Mild Bill, ghost bullets do just fine against the undead."

"I'm a zombie, not a ghost," I said. "There's a difference."

Moondance McClantock frowned, as if he hadn't considered that. I glanced over at Sheyenne, who waited at the boardwalk. She spread her hands, clearly not knowing the answer. The ghost gunslingers didn't know either.

Robin marched over to stand close to me, her expression stern. "You all have to stop this, right now. It's against the law."

Seeing that all of the vengeful ghost gunslingers had drawn their weapons, I urgently pushed her out of the way. "McGoo, get her out of here. I don't want either of you in the line of fire. Robin's been lucky enough once today."

She tried to argue, but McGoo didn't. Though she resisted, he escorted her toward the boardwalk.

As soon as they were three steps away, Moondance McClantock and his gang lifted their revolvers, ready to gun me down. The ghost gunslingers aimed their weapons at me, and the staccato sound of twelve hammers being cocked back sounded like a high-caliber rattlesnake.

I was standing there all by myself in the middle of the street, arms loose at my sides—or as loose as a zombie's arms could be. I held my .38 in my right hand, but how could that stand against six pairs of six-shooters full of ghost bullets? Besides, my real bullets would just pass through the outlaw apparitions, but the ghost bullets were not likely to pass harmlessly through me.

As the tension ratcheted up, the town clock started bonging again—apparently the previous bells had just been a warm-up for high midnight. It all happened very quickly.

Just as they all opened fire at their target of a lone, and hopefully brave, zombie detective standing in the middle of the main street, McGoo let out a shout and threw himself in front of me like a human shield, flailing his arms. The twelve ghostly Colts roared with the sound of thunder.

From the boardwalk, Sheyenne and Robin both screamed.

In instant reaction, I managed *not* to fire my .38—a good thing, or I would have shot my Best Human Friend in the back, and he was already facing a storm of bullets from Moondance McClantock and his gang. The gunfire went on and on until the outlaws emptied their revolvers into my friend.

I expected McGoo to drop lifeless to the ground. Instead, he stood there and turned to look at me in astonishment. "Well, that was one of the stupidest things I've ever done."

Robin bounded into the street, grabbing McGoo's shirt, patting him down, looking for the dozens of bullet holes. But there were none.

He showed me a nervous, relieved grin while the ghost gunslingers gaped at him, surprised and annoyed. "I guess I'm smarter than I thought I was," McGoo said. "I figured it out, Shamble. Robin wasn't just lucky earlier, and she didn't dodge the bullets when Deadeye One-Eye gunned down Mild Bill. Ghost bullets can kill ghosts, but they don't harm normal people, in the same way that normal bullets don't harm ghosts."

I still couldn't believe he was intact. "That was an awfully idiotic way to test a theory, McGoo."

"You wanted me to think it through for a day or two? I didn't really have the time to do my due diligence. I had to act right away." He patted his chest again, just in case he had missed a few dozen bullet holes.

I felt a lump in my throat, and it wasn't from anything nasty I had swallowed. "Thanks, McGoo. You saved me."

Moondance McClantock shouted, "Reload, boys! Time for round two."

Now Robin stormed forward, striding down the main street toward the ghost gunslingers. I could tell by That Look on her face that she was angry now, really angry— and no one got in Robin Deyer's way when she was angry. "Oh, no you don't!" She faced the twelve six-guns, and even if she hadn't already seen proof that ghost bullets couldn't harm her, I think she would have walked right up to surly gunslingers regardless. "You are not allowed."

Robin's handbag was actually more of a satchel for legal documents, and she had been working with Mild Bill's ghost until the very opening of the Wild West Show. Now she reached into her satchel and yanked out a folded document, waving it in the faces of the ghost gunslingers. "Holster your guns. You are not allowed—it says right here."

McClantock guffawed. "Oh, little lady! So now you're the lawman?"

"Not the lawman," Robin said with a sniff. "I am *the law*. Legal contracts. You signed this yourself."

"Not me." McClantock adjusted his turquoise bracelets and straightened his bolo tie. "That was our agent."

"And he has power of attorney. It's signed in blood."

"Not our blood, borrowed blood."

"It's still legally binding. The terms specifically state 'a limited engagement, one and only one exhibition of gunplay.' Your agent was very specific, and a ruthless negotiator. You all insisted on the terms." She jabbed her fingers at the contract. "You emptied your guns. You shot at your target. Therefore your legal obligations have been satisfied. You are no longer allowed to fire any bullets at Mr. Chambeaux, whether for vengeance or for entertainment purposes. You cannot rescind the contract."

"That's ridiculous," said McClantock. "That wasn't the spirit of the contract."

"It's the letter of the law," Robin said.

The gunslinger with the big beard and big eyebrows

said, "Better be careful, boss—we don't want our agent to dump us."

Deadeye One-Eye groaned in disgust. "Why do you think I went freelance? I've told you guys over and over that you have to read your contracts! It's your own damn fault."

Sensing there was more fun to be had at the Wild West Show even after the gunfire, the skittish crowd began to reappear. Apparently they had shut off the water in their bathtubs, checked on their pets, stirred the burning casserole on the stove, and whatever other excuses they had made to get out of the danger zone.

The unkempt gunslinger ghosts stood, grumbling. They gathered around Robin's copy of the contract, scrutinizing the clauses again and again to find some loophole—which was difficult, as many of them were illiterate.

The ghost of Mild Bill's ghost shimmered in the air before them. He clapped his hands and grinned at the spectators. "Show's not over yet, folks! Lots more fun all through the night."

Albert the ghoul began picking up dust-encrusted remnants of his barbecued bones scattered over the ground. He inspected them with a drooping, milky eye, painted more sauce over the dirt, and offered them for sale again.

Still muttering, Moondance McClantock tucked the folded copy of the contract in his vest, and then all the ghost gunslingers vanished into the darkness.

Sheyenne ran forward from the boardwalk, looking restored now. The ectoplasmic blood in her makeshift bandage had faded. I cocked my fedora and said in a completely unconvincing drawl, "You look pretty as a picture, Miss Sheyenne." Then I turned to Mild Bill's ghost. "Show's over for us. We've had enough of this sort of entertainment. I prefer something a little more noir."

McGoo was already telling tall tales to the enthusiastic audience members, and I let him have his day in the moonlight. His selfless bravery had certainly touched me.

But when the crowd congratulated me on my victory over the ghost outlaws, insisting that they'd really wanted to help, if it weren't for so many other obligations—I didn't want to hear the excuses. I wondered how great-great umpty-ump grandpappy Marshal Dirk Chambeaux had felt in the Old West facing outlaws and bank robbers.

"Too bad we can't just ride off into the sunset," Sheyenne said. I felt a tingle as she slipped a ghostly arm through mine.

I shook my head. "No way—sunset is when things start hopping in the Unnatural Quarter."

"Then let's get hopping," she said.

Together, we all left the cursed Indian burial ground, looking for a good time on our own.

Collector's Curse

When my ghost girlfriend Sheyenne and I went to a quirky estate sale, we didn't expect to find horrific murders caused by nefarious curses. That's not what you usually encounter at estate sales, which are filled with oddities, antiques, furniture, and unusual leftovers from a person's life. At least we did find some bargains and collectibles, too.

The estate sale tables covered the poorly maintained yard of a poorly maintained shuttered-up house in a quiet neighborhood. After all the monsters had returned to the world in the event known as the Big Uneasy, many of them eventually settled down in conventional residential areas in the Unnatural Quarter.

Eldon Muff was a crotchety, bitter old werewolf who had bought the ramshackle house in the turbulent days immediately after the Big Uneasy, when real estate prices dropped dramatically. Some might say he'd paid a song for it, but Eldon had no interest in songs, or music, or any entertainment whatsoever. He had lived alone and died alone, never married—which was no surprise at all to anyone who had ever spent more than five minutes with him. Even harpies from a paid dating service refused to go out with Eldon more than once.

Fortunately, as a zombie detective, I had never worked with Eldon, though he constantly threatened to sue anyone who had slighted him. He spouted every conspiracy meme he saw on social media (even the ones insisting that such memes were themselves a conspiracy to make people doubt conspiracy theories). My Best Human Friend, Officer Toby McGoohan, had dealt with many of Eldon's complaints though, and McGoo often stopped by our offices just to blow off steam whenever he dealt with the surly old werewolf.

Eldon had filed formal complaints against the paperboy for harassing him (by ringing his doorbell and trying to collect the months-overdue subscription), or when a young lycanthropic hooligan continually crept onto his property to urinate on the bushes, marking his territory as dogs will often do. No matter how loudly Eldon howled, "Get off my lawn!" the werewolf teenager kept coming back, clearly entertained by Eldon's impotent fury. No, the old werewolf had not made many friends.

Now that he was dead, all of his neighbors came out to pick over his possessions, looking at the display tables strewn with ridiculous and useless items, but trying to haggle down the prices nevertheless.

Sheyenne and I thought it would be a fine excuse for a date, just a zombie P.I. and a ghost out for an afternoon stroll. We enjoyed observing the curiosity seekers who picked over the jelly jar glasses, the hideous clock in the rounded belly of a laughing Buddhist monk, a lava lamp with real lava now hardened into dull black lumps, a folding kitchen table with room enough for one, decks of playing cards that had only been used for games of solitaire, and folded clothing that exuded an "old man" smell.

"Tell me if you see anything you like, Spooky," I said.

Sheyenne's spectral brow furrowed. "Don't hold your breath."

She was far more beautiful than I deserved. As a ghost, she couldn't touch me, and our romance faced a few challenges due to intangibility, but we did our best. She had been alive when we started dating, as was I, but sometimes relationships take an unexpected turn. Today I wore my usual brown sport jacket with the clumsily stitched bullet holes across the front, and I tilted my fedora in place, though not enough to cover the bullet hole in the middle of my forehead. It was a reminder of how I'd been killed on a case.

I picked up a classic metal lunchbox from the old TV show, *The Munsters*, which, after the Big Uneasy, was now viewed as an insightful family drama. Next to it were packs of *Twilight Zone* trading cards, never opened, with bubblegum petrified so hard it was beyond the ability of even a shark-jawed demon to chew. The tables were full of similar nostalgic stuff.

"Sure is a lot of junk," I said.

"Some would call them rarities and collectibles," said a frizzy-furred gremlin who bustled up, hoping she could catch my interest. I recognized Rita, a savvy gremlin businesswoman who had taken over her brother's pawn shop after his unfortunate murder. Rita was running the estate sale.

"We're just looking," I replied. "I'm not much of a collector."

"We are bargain hunters, though," Sheyenne said and moved on to another table.

Eldon Muff was more than a collector or bargain hunter, though. He'd been a hoarder, but since he kept his shades drawn and his doors locked, and never had company over, no one really understood the extent of his fervor. I couldn't imagine how all these possessions spread on table after table across the yard, filling the garage, the driveway, and the sidewalk could possibly fit inside one small rundown house, but the old werewolf must have packed every corner and every room, wall to ceiling.

Unfortunately, his overzealous collecting led to his demise. Eldon collected possessions like he collected grudges, but apparently he didn't organize either one very well. The old werewolf had been buried under a mountain of discontinued monster Hummel figurines still in their original boxes. The cute but disturbing miniature figures of charming slack-faced ghouls and rotting zombies hadn't found the right audience. Eldon had bought the whole truckload, also presumably for a song, but he had stacked the pile of original boxes too high, and they fell over and crushed him. An unknown amount of time later, the insistent young zombie paperboy had come yet again to collect on the overdue subscription fee and found him dead. The withered, half-rotted werewolf looked decidedly less cute than even the least cute of the monster Hummel figurines.

Eldon Muff had no heirs, not even any friends, but a new bulldozing company was eager to buy his house so they could use it for employee practice—hence, the reason for this complete life-liquidation sale. I hoped that at least the unpaid zombie paperboy would receive part of the proceeds for his overdue bill.

Curious, I went to a rack of shelves crammed with old paperback books, the kind with red edges and garish artwork, 50¢ cover price. They looked to be in mint condition. They caught my eye because they were detective novels, at least three dozen of them. A grin crept across my cold gray face.

"Look at these, Spooky. They're classics by John D. MacDonald. I love his detective Travis McGee." I pulled out three at random. *Nightmare in Pink, A Purple Place for Dying, Free Fall in Crimson.*

Sheyenne snuggled close, and I felt the tingling aura of her insubstantial yet curvaceous body. I said, "Reading old detective novels is what inspired me to be a private investigator. Well, that and not being able to make it through police academy." It was a constant embarrassment to know that McGoo was better at criminal academics than I was.

I called out to the gremlin running the sale. "How much are the paperbacks, Rita?"

The fuzzy woman glanced up from wrapping a complete set of Flintstones shot glasses. "Fifty cents each."

I considered, glancing at Sheyenne. "These were my

favorites." I looked at the three old paperbacks, then pondered the entire collection.

"You don't have time to read, Beaux," Sheyenne reminded me. "You have too many cases."

"Maybe they'll serve as inspiration," I said, deciding to take the three, but not the whole set. Sheyenne went over to look at the varied kitchen utensils, even though as a ghost she couldn't eat, nor did she spend much time cooking. I happily paid for my three books.

As I opened the first paperback, *Nightmare in Pink*, I was surprised to discover handwriting inside. When I realized that the books were signed, I felt like a game show contestant who had unexpectedly won a bonus round. But when I flipped to the title page I discovered not John D. MacDonald's autograph, but the much-less-collectible scrawl of the old werewolf, words written in angry, hard strokes. "I hereby curse the paperboy Bobby Neumann for his incessant harassment. When this curse is activated, he shall die a truly horrible death. My vengeance extends beyond the grave! Sincerely yours, Eldon Muff."

The crotchety werewolf sure did know how to hold a grudge. Curious, I opened the second of the three paperbacks, *A Purple Place for Dying*, and also found Muff's handwriting there. "I hereby curse the vile Reginald Dinkler for constantly peeing on my shrubs. When this curse is activated, he shall die a truly horrible death. My vengeance extends beyond the grave! Sincerely yours, Eldon Muff."

I looked at the shelf filled with dozens more paperbacks. I guess the hairy old recluse needed some way to spend his time. I wondered if all the books contained a similar curse.

Before I could check them out, however, a thin and dusty mummy shuffled up to the rack of books, studying them with his extended fingers. His bandages were yellowish-brown except for a few swaddles of fresh white gauze where he had patched himself up. His entire head was covered, including his eyes, leaving him blind. He ran his gnarled fingertips along the spines of the paperbacks. "Wonderful. Ah, just wonderful!" he muttered, his voice dry and dusty. "They're in perfect condition." He drew in a long breath. "Mint."

I stepped closer. "I don't have a mint, but I have gum," I offered, quickly realizing that the old mummy needed it.

"No, I mean these books. They're pristine and highly collectible. I want the complete set."

"I already bought three of them," I said, holding up the ones I had taken. "And how can you read? You don't have eyes."

"I don't need eyes to appreciate fine collectibles," the mummy said. "Don't you know who I am?"

"Actually, I don't," I said, and extended my hand. "I'm Dan Chambeaux, zombie private investigator. I'd give you one of my cards, but it wouldn't do you much good."

"I'll remember," said the mummy. "I am Ro-Tar, known since the time of ancient Egypt."

"Most mummies I know come from ancient Egypt," I said, although I had met a few Inca and Aztec mummies. "Normally, the mummification job is a little better. Did they make a mistake preserving your eyes?"

Ro-Tar seemed ashamed. He bent his bandaged head. "Yes, and dozens suffered the same fate. Caused by an improperly trained embalming employee. There was a class action suit." He turned his bandaged, eyeless face toward me. "But my legacy remains. I created a very popular luncheon club for business networking and guest speakers. It was named after me, and it still endures."

"Oh, yes. I've heard of the Rotarians. I didn't know their origin, though."

"Now I'm retired," said the mummy, making me wonder about the retirement age for someone who was thousands of years old. "And I'm an avid collector. I simply must have these paperbacks." He waved his bandaged hand to get Rita's attention. "How much for the books?"

"Two dollars each," the gremlin said without taking a breath. I held on to my three 50¢ paperbacks and didn't point out the price difference.

"Sold! I'll take the lot," Ro-Tar said and cackled in a low voice to me. "She has no idea what these are worth."

Sheyenne called, "Beaux, look what I found!" She lifted several colorful lacy scarves that fell more into the lingerie category than hold-your-hair-against-the-wind category.

Finding my beautiful girlfriend more interesting than old paperbacks, I helped her select several veils that I thought would look best on her. She lifted them with her poltergeist powers, and the wispy fabric drifted around her insubstantial form. I had no idea how or why mangy old Eldon Muff used the sexy scarves, nor did I want to know. What I did care about, though, was how pretty they were going to look on Sheyenne.

Ro-Tar, the blind mummy, was carefully packing his entire collection of pristine paperbacks into his sarcophagus, which had a set of wheels for easier carrying. I tucked my three books under my arm, but frankly my attention was on how Sheyenne would model the colorful scarves later in private.

Back at Chambeaux & Deyer Investigations, Sheyenne used her supernatural skills to organize our office, a task that exceeded the abilities of any mere human.

Robin, my lovely and talented lawyer partner, was busy in her own office preparing notes for an upcoming trial. She was defending a shapeless oily blob that left ugly stains wherever it went. The client had been charged with damage to public property, but Robin's defense was that the blob had a right to exhibit free expression and artistic verve. Regardless of this defense, Sheyenne adamantly refused to let the greasy blob creature into our offices because of the possible damage to our carpets.

The office phone rang before I had a chance to slump into my office chair, where I planned to stare at the folders of unsolved cases. I often expected clues to jump out at me like a cat from a dark alley in a bad horror movie. When I heard McGoo on the line, I realized I should have bought some junk from the estate sale to give him as a thoughtful birthday gift.

"Hey, Shamble—want to see a particularly nasty crime scene? I mean really gross and unbelievable? The victim must have had the worst karma of any person on Earth, off the charts bloody and tragic." He was trying to make it sound like a selling point.

"I'll be right there. You need my help solving it?"

"Not much of a mystery, but this is one for the record books."

I met him at the crime scene just outside of the opera house. The Unnatural Quarter wasn't known for extravagant cultural events, but the Phantom did reasonably well at the opera, especially with his Saturday afternoon children's matinees and with his midnight laser light shows, all accompanied by pipe organ music.

Crime scene techs had placed yellow tape around a splattered bloody mess that looked like a meat delivery truck had crashed into a shipment of plumbing supplies. Gore and polished pipes were scattered around amongst ivory keys that looked like long rectangular teeth.

I looked up and saw a snapped rope dangling from the pulley near the roof of the opera house, and I realized that these weren't plumbing supplies, but polished pieces of one of the Phantom's grand pipe organs. A bent kid's bicycle lay crashed in the gutter.

Being a detective, even a zombie detective, I didn't need a calculator to put two and two together. The rope hoisting the large pipe organ up to the rooftop level of the opera house had broken, and the huge organ had toppled onto some poor victim on the street. The pipes had fallen straight down and punched through the body like an automated press that mass-produced hamburger patties. Goblin evidence technicians kept busy sorting the mess into tubular debris and mangled-flesh debris, often using tweezers.

"You weren't kidding, McGoo. This is pretty gross."

In front of the building, the Phantom strutted about in his tuxedo, looking distraught. He pulled off the white porcelain mask that covered half of his face, wiped sweat from his ugly visage, and popped the mask back into place. "That was one of my best organs, too."

"It made quite a crash when all those pipes clanged and clattered onto the sidewalk," McGoo said. "Nobody even heard the poor kid scream, although half of the neighbors are now deaf."

"Being deaf might help them enjoy the opera better," I said.

McGoo nodded, as if he hadn't considered that before. He's a redheaded beat cop with a round freckle-spattered face and a grin full of humor that often gets him in trouble. He'd been transferred from a normal precinct to work in the Unnatural Quarter because of his unfortunate penchant for telling politically incorrect jokes.

As he paced around the crime scene tape, looking at the wreckage, the Phantom frowned with the unmasked half of his face. "If the pipes aren't too dented, maybe we can reassemble the whole thing. I don't know about the sound quality, but we could advertise that it's a blood-cursed organ. Imagine the tickets we'd sell."

I looked up at the snapped rope high above. "Why were you hoisting the organ up to the rooftop level?"

"Special springtime event," he said. "We were going to have an open-air barbecue. Hamburgers and hot dogs along with opera. We thought it might catch the lowbrow audience."

"Free hot dogs," McGoo said. "That might even get me listening to opera."

Something still didn't seem right to me about this crime scene. It was too improbable. I saw a couple of burly blue-collar golems standing next to the other end of the broken rope, looking confused because they obviously hadn't finished their job. They had been standing here, using brute force to pull the rope and raise the organ from the sidewalk up to the roof.

"So where did the organ come from in the first place? You were moving it from where to where?"

"It started out in the second-floor gallery," the Phantom said. "We brought it down here and out onto the sidewalk, so the golems could lift it up to the roof."

"And how did it get onto the sidewalk in the first place?"

The Phantom turned to me as if wondering why I was so interested in the mechanics of furniture moving. "The golems carried it out of the second-floor gallery down the stairs onto the street, where they tied the ropes and began hauling it up to the third story, where we could swing it into the attic and then carry it up to the roof."

"But if it was already in the second-floor gallery, why didn't they just carry it up the third flight of stairs?"

The Phantom shrugged, turned to the golems. "Union rules, I think."

I looked at the mangled mess of what had been some poor unlucky kid on a bicycle. "I guess he was just in the wrong place at the wrong time."

The Phantom clucked his tongue. "He shouldn't have been here at all. I don't even subscribe to his newspaper, and I've tried again and again to stop the kid from throwing papers in front of my opera house. Somebody has to pick them up, and nobody reads them."

"A paperboy?" I asked, suddenly alert.

McGoo said, "Yeah, I guess his name was Bobby Neumann, a zombie kid." He shook his head. "Black and white and red all over, that's for sure."

Bobby Neumann ... I knew that name. I suddenly realized it was the same zombie paperboy who had found Eldon Muff dead in his home buried under a pile of monster Hummel figurines. "That's quite a coincidence."

McGoo raised his eyebrows. "You subscribed to the same paper, Shamble?"

"No, not that." I started to explain about the estate sale, but before I got to the part about the curse written inside the old paperback, McGoo received a call on his police radio.

"1063A just occurred at the Gardening and Cemetery Supply Center. It's a 1616 with a 793C."

Around the mess in front of the Phantom's opera house the crime techs also picked up their phones, studied the information, and got ready to move.

McGoo clicked his radio, and his face looked as gray as mine normally did. "Oh, no. Is it a 71B or a 71C?"

The dispatcher hesitated. "71C, I'm afraid."

He groaned. "Oh, this is bad."

Even though I had spent a few years at the police academy before deciding to get my private investigator's license, I hadn't kept up on all the new crime scene codes. Even so, I felt an odd dread build in my stomach. "I missed some of that, McGoo. What happened, exactly?"

"An awful accident at the home and garden center," he said. "A salesman was demonstrating different models of lawnmowers used to trim cemetery plots. Some teenage werewolf kid had just gotten a job at Greenlawn Cemetery and was there admiring the equipment." He swallowed hard. "But a drunk poltergeist somehow got lost inside the engine of the lawnmower that was being demonstrated, and the demon-possessed gardening machine went berserk. It mowed right over the poor werewolf kid." He shook his head. "Unfortunately, the blades were set to golf course level, so it trimmed the victim's fur all the way down to his internal organs."

I was amazed that McGoo could have gotten so many details from the code numbers in the police call. "Another truly horrible death. What was the victim's name? The werewolf boy?"

"He was eighteen, so not really a boy, like Bobby Neumann." McGoo glanced over at the mangled pipe organ and the bloody mess on the sidewalk. He asked the dispatcher, who responded, "His name was Reginald Dinkler."

Seeing my shocked look, McGoo said, "Did you know him?"

"I read his name in a book. And Bobby Neumann, too."

I narrowed my eyes, settled my fedora more firmly on my head, because I was going to have to do a lot of thinking as a zombie P.I. "These aren't just accidents. We've got a curse on our hands."

Back in the office, feeling the urgency, I went straight to my desk and picked up the three old paperbacks I'd purchased from the estate sale. I spread them out on the conference room table while McGoo, Robin, and Sheyenne gathered, curious. "Eldon Muff was a thoroughly unpleasant man," I said, "but now I have proof that he was actively evil."

"That old werewolf hated everyone," Robin said. "It's been documented."

"Yes, and he particularly hated the paperboy and the teenage werewolf who peed on his shrubs. He wrote a curse in these two paperbacks." I picked up *Nightmare in Pink* and read Eldon's scrawled writing. "I hereby curse the paperboy Bobby Neumann for his incessant harassment. When this curse is activated, he shall die a truly horrible death. My vengeance extends beyond the grave! Sincerely yours, Eldon Muff."

"Well that does sound suspicious," said McGoo. He had followed me from the crime scene, not understanding what some used paperbacks had to do with horrifically mangled accident victims, although he did admit how much he enjoyed John D. MacDonald's detective novels.

"Being killed by a plummeting pipe organ counts as a horrible death," Sheyenne said.

"And here's the second one." I read aloud the curse from *A Purple Place for Dying*, which identified Reginald Dinkler as the lucky recipient.

I rested my gray-skinned hand on the third book, *Free Fall in Crimson*, holding it closed. "I haven't looked in this one yet."

"But Eldon died some time ago," Sheyenne said. "Why did the curses activate now? This afternoon?"

"I think I triggered them by opening the books and reading the words."

Robin frowned at the old paperbacks. Her brown-eyed stare was intense, and I could see the legal wheels turning in her mind. She had given up a chance at a far more lucrative corporate law practice to see that unnaturals got justice after the Big Uneasy.

McGoo snorted. "Are you suggesting that you're responsible? That the paperboy and the werewolf urinator are dead because you wanted to do a little recreational reading? Whew, I'm glad I don't read much."

"Stranger things have happened," I said.

McGoo scratched his head. "Not many that I can think of." I could probably come up with a few after all my cases, but I didn't want to encourage what would certainly be a lengthy and pointless discussion.

I picked up *Free Fall in Crimson*. "There's one way to find out. If Eldon wrote another curse inside this book, we'll know the target. He always names his victims." I looked at McGoo. "Once the curse is activated, we should have a little time. Do you think you could rally the UQPD fast enough to put protection around the target, whoever or whatever it is?"

McGoo straightened his blue cap on his head. "If we start the paperwork now."

Sheyenne looked nervous. "What if this causes another murder, Beaux?"

"Another *accident*," Robin corrected. "Legally speaking, Dan can't be held responsible since he didn't place the curse. It's clearly not his handwriting."

"I don't want to cause another grisly death," I said, tapping the paperback. "But the curse exists, and it could be triggered anytime the book is opened."

"We could just burn the book," McGoo suggested. "Wouldn't that cancel the curse?"

"I don't like the precedent of book burning," Robin said.

Sheyenne and I both reacted with alarm. I said, "I don't want to mess with curses. There could be nasty unintended consequences, and the horror could spread. If we activate the curse under our own terms, though, at least this way we can respond and try to help the poor victim."

I looked at Robin, then at Sheyenne. Both of them showed their support. McGoo sighed and took out his police radio. "I'll call it in as soon as we know, just to make sure."

Since I'd just had a fresh embalming treatment last week, my fingers were more nimble than usual. I opened the cover of *Free Fall in Crimson*, turned to the title page, and spotted Eldon's angry handwriting. Bracing myself, I read aloud, "I hereby curse Nolan Pratt for his incompetence as a house painter. He left thin spots on my eastern wall, didn't clean up his mess, overcharged me, and never cleaned out the gutters as he promised. When this curse is activated, he shall die a truly horrible death. My vengeance extends beyond the grave! Sincerely yours, Eldon Muff."

I lurched to my feet, and I'm very good at lurching. "We've got to find this Nolan Pratt and keep him safe."

McGoo was already calling in the report over his police radio. "Send a protective detail right away!" When the dispatcher asked for details, he replied, "We don't know what's going to happen. It's a curse! A meteor could fall from the sky for all I know. Just find Pratt and keep him safe. We're on our way."

We all rushed out of the office together.

The curse-prevention response was a military-style operation, like a sophisticated army sweeping in to conquer a small country. The headquarters of Pratt House Painting & Bell Maintenance was just a little office in a business park with one receptionist who had no idea what was happening. She was a fluttery ghost of an old woman who nearly disassociated from fright when she saw the invasion.

"We're a protective detail," McGoo announced as he and I rushed in, accompanied by Sheyenne, Robin, and half of the UQPD. Everyone was armed to the teeth, and many of them were unnaturals with extravagant teeth, too.

The old receptionist nearly faded away. "But Nolan's not here. He's out on a job."

"Where is he? We need the address," I said. "His life's in danger."

"He's cursed," Robin said, as if it were a legal term.

The receptionist was so flustered she lost control of her poltergeist powers. Fortunately, as a ghost, she didn't need to worry about losing control of her bladder, which she might well have done, considering the panicked expression on her face. The woman fumbled with her intangible hands but couldn't manage to touch the pages in the appointment calendar. Finally, Sheyenne flitted in and helped her find the location of the painter's current day job.

Armed with the address, our curse-protective detail left the business office and moved our invasion elsewhere, hoping to get to the unsuspecting victim in time.

Nolan Pratt was a broad-shouldered hunchback with shaggy hair, a paint-spattered baseball cap and paint-spattered overalls. He had been contracted to paint a two-story residence with a small but nice front yard, in which he had posted a small sign that said, "Painting Courtesy of Pratt House Painting & Bell Maintenance."

Instead of using a ladder, Nolan preferred to dangle from the roof on ropes, swinging about as if he were high up in a belfry somewhere. He hung suspended on the rope harness holding a bucket of paint in one hand and a wide brush in the other. He swung back and forth in pendular arcs, slathering strokes of paint across the house's siding, covering areas in curves rather than straight lines. He missed quite a few spots.

As the fleet of squad cars pulled up to the house with their lights flashing and sirens wailing, the hunchback spilled the bucket of paint down the siding, which actually provided better coverage than his brush had done. He dangled in panic, trapped in the rope harness. McGoo and I led the swarm of the protective detail in a mad dash to rescue the victim, although in his panic Nolan lost his footing and nearly hung himself.

The UQPD came in heavily armed, some with revolvers, some with sniper rifles, others with batons or tear gas canisters. McGoo and I drew our respective pistols ready to shoot anything on sight. "We're here to keep you safe," I said.

"House painting isn't really that dangerous," the hunchback replied.

"Get down from there, sir," McGoo said. "Now! For your own protection."

Terrified into cooperating, Nolan extricated himself from the harness and ropes, then sprang to the ground, bouncing on bent legs. "What's all this about?"

"You're cursed," I said. "Eldon Muff wants you to meet with a horrible death—and soon."

"We all wanted that hairy old fart to meet a horrible death." The hunchback snorted. "All my other clients are satisfied. Just look at my rating with the Better Business Bureau."

"This is one of those rare cases where customer satisfaction doesn't count," I said. "Eldon died and left a curse, with you as a specific target. Two other victims have already suffered horrible deaths, a persistent paperboy and a shrub urinator."

The hunchback's expression pinched into one of distaste. "I thought I smelled something in those shrubs." I was surprised he could smell anything, since he reeked of turpentine and sweat.

As I started to describe the curse, a whistling sound came from high above. We all looked up to see a glittering object plummeting straight toward us, straight toward the house, no doubt straight toward the hunchback painter.

"Look out!" I yelled. "Everybody out of the way!"

Even though it sounded ridiculous, McGoo had, in fact, mentioned the possibility of a meteor falling from the sky. Either forgetting or not understanding the concept of protecting someone, the protective detail bolted like cockroaches exposed to the light.

I tackled the hunchback, knocking him into the middle of the lawn an instant before a tumbling blue-white object crashed into the freshly painted side of the house, exactly where Nolan Pratt had been dangling only moments before. The irregular hunk of blue ice broke in shards studded with smeared swatches of paper and frozen oblong brown lumps.

The terrified hunchback picked himself up and stared in astonishment. Sheyenne's ghost swooped close to make sure I was all right. I climbed back to my feet, brushed off my sport jacket, and adjusted my fedora. McGoo and the protective detail came running back, now that it was safe.

Robin stepped up to the broken frozen debris, which had left a crater in the front yard. She looked at it analytically. "Is it a meteor? A comet?"

"Something worse," I said. I had heard about these hazards before but had never seen one with my own eyes. "It's a frozen ball dumped from an airplane toilet reservoir, a block of ice from the sky. They usually don't make it to the ground, but I guess this was a bigger lump than usual."

"I could've been killed!" Nolan cried.

"And in a most unsanitary way," I said.

Sheyenne drifted close, wrapping her intangible arms around me. "That was close!"

"Is it over now?" McGoo asked. "Did we break the curse?"

"We need to have the curses studied by an expert," Robin said, "but from my preliminary analysis in the legal library, those handwritten curses are inexpensive, one-time-only curses."

"Eldon Muff was very frugal," McGoo agreed.

The hunchback adjusted his paint-spattered baseball cap and looked at the ruined side of the house, not to mention the crater and the blue toilet ice in the front yard. "The customer isn't going to be happy about that, but they signed a specific waiver absolving me of responsibility for meteor strikes."

Robin's brow furrowed. "They might have legal grounds to contest it, sir. A frozen ball of ice and turds from an airplane isn't technically a meteor." When the hunchback looked distraught, she reassured him, "If it comes to that, I'll take the case as your defense attorney."

I felt relieved to see the house painter safe and sound, frazzled but unsoiled by the fecal comet. "We couldn't save Bobby and Reginald from their horrible deaths, but least we saved Mr. Pratt. And those were the only three curses." I decided never to open the MacDonald paperbacks again.

Then I froze, remembering that the blind mummy had bought dozens more at the estate sale, and I had no doubt that each one of those books held a similar curse.

Leaving the UQPD army to clean up the unfortunate residence and lock down the crime scene, McGoo and I commandeered one of the squad cars and raced off to Ro-Tar's house. Robin and Sheyenne joined us, while the rest of the protective detail remained on call, eager for over-time should we need them.

We recognized the mummy's quaint, well-maintained abode by the large Rotarian sign in the front yard. Racing from the parked squad car, we pounded on the front door, urgently yelled the mummy's name, and soon we heard the shuffle-slide of his wrapped footsteps as he came to answer the knock.

When he opened the door, Ro-Tar had fresh bandages wrapped around his eyes like a blindfold. He also wore a stylish paisley smoking jacket, and I was very afraid of what might happen if a burning cigarette touched his flam-mable bandages. On the bright side, the gauze over his mouth would have filtered the smoke, thereby reducing the carcinogenic hazard.

I blurted out, "We're here about all those collectible paperbacks you bought at the estate sale. They're cursed!"

"We have to confiscate them," McGoo said. "They're already responsible for two deaths and one ruined house painting job."

The blind mummy recognized my voice. "The books are collector's editions, Mr. Chambeaux, and they're not for sale. They are extremely valuable."

"But you don't understand," Sheyenne said. "People are going to die."

The mummy sniffed through empty nasal sockets. "They are murder mysteries, after all."

He politely led us inside his home, which was like a museum. The furniture was distinctly art deco. Framed prints and old movie posters hung on the walls, and shelves and curio cabinets covered the rest of the space. Every inch was crammed with collectibles, eccentric memorabilia from old radio programs, promotional items from long-cancelled TV shows, framed original comic panels. His best items, including the set of classic paperbacks, were stored in magnificent cherrywood bookshelves fronted with locked glass cabinet doors, as if he feared the books might take wing and escape.

"I just displayed all those fine John D. MacDonald paperbacks. Here's the entire collection." Ro-Tar stood in front of the glass-enclosed book case, though he couldn't see the contents. "They are absolutely pristine."

"But you can't read them," Robin said. "You have no eyes."

"I have eye sockets. And I can appreciate fine rare books."

I looked at all the spines lined up inside the case, nearly fifty of them. Each paperback had been lovingly sealed in a separate protective plastic bag, then arranged in order behind the transparent cabinet doors.

"We think that each one of those books contains a terrible curse," McGoo said. "If you open them, people will die horrible deaths."

"*Open* them?" Ro-Tar said, recoiling in a different sort of horror. "I wouldn't even touch them! They're protected and preserved, sealed away on display."

"But if you ever read them, you will activate the curse," Robin said.

"Read them!" the mummy scoffed. "They're collector's books! They're not meant to be read, merely to be owned, merely to be coveted." He was growing vehement. "And I will not let you have them. They're perfectly safe with me."

"But if someone—" I began.

"I can assure you, they will never be read, Mr. Chambeaux," Ro-Tar replied. "They'll never be touched. I'll allow no fingerprints on the covers. The spines will never be cracked."

"Then we don't have to worry about the curse being triggered," I said, but I remained curious. "If you don't ever intend to read them, why are you so fascinated with the books?"

"Because I *have* them," Ro-Tar said so vehemently that he coughed dust out of his mouth bandages. "And for a collector, that's the most important thing."

McGoo remained indignant. "Those items are extremely dangerous. We have to take them back to the police station, store them safely in the evidence room."

I had seen the chaos of the UQPD evidence room. More than once, spell-contaminated items had gone missing, sacred amulets had been misfiled, immortality elixirs spilled in birth certificate files. In contrast, I looked around at the mummy's absolutely pristine and well-maintained collection, the plastic seals on the cursed books, the locked cabinet.

"On second thought, McGoo, these cursed books might be in better hands if they just stay locked up here."

"They will never be in any hands at all," Ro-Tar said. "No one will ever touch them!"

"Exactly what I mean," I said. "We'll know where they are, but the deadly curses will remain sealed. Forever."

"Nothing is forever," Ro-Tar said philosophically, as if it were something he had once heard from a Rotarian luncheon speaker. "But I've been around for thousands of years, and I know how to take care of valuable old things."

Though she remained concerned, Robin came to the same conclusion I had. After considering all the paperwork required to file and maintain each one of these cursed books, signing them into evidence, and then keeping them completely secure, without mishap, McGoo agreed with my assessment. "Sounds like the best curse prevention we can manage."

Pleased to have visitors, now that we could breathe a sigh of relief about the looming curses, Ro-Tar took the time to show us around his fascinating collection. I became more and more convinced this was a more stable and protected place than the UQPD evidence room. Maybe I could convince McGoo to transfer a few other dangerous artifacts ...

When we were ready to go, I said to Sheyenne, "Maybe we'd better avoid estate sales from now on."

"Never again," my ghost girlfriend agreed. "But you don't want me to return all those veils and lingerie, do you?"

"Not just yet," I said. I was looking forward to seeing her model them for me. "They may be collector's items."

Wishful Thinking

I

I hate to see a werewolf cry. The tears and the sniffles make the facial fur all matted and clumpy, and the despairing whimper sounds like a little lap dog trying to growl.

"New client, Beaux," Sheyenne whispered, hovering at my office door, "and she's a nervous wreck." My ghost girlfriend is a curvaceous blond with sparkling blue eyes and a glowing ectoplasmic presence. She lowered her voice. "You'd better come out in person, and quick."

I sat behind my cluttered desk piled with folders of unsolved cases as well as unpaid bills from clients. As a zombie private detective, I sometimes have dead afternoons, and other times I can't keep up with the action. I rose on my stiff joints and followed Sheyenne out into the receiving area of Chambeaux & Deyer Investigations.

A frumpy, middle-aged werewolf woman stood there in a floral print housedress, sobbing. She'd already been through four wadded facial tissues from the box on the desk, but her long black claws had shredded the paper, even as she sniffled and blew her dark nose.

"There, there, ma'am." I used my best You can trust me, I'm a detective voice. "We'll help you with your problem, whatever it is. I'm back from the dead and back on the case." It was my catchphrase, and often it impressed the unnatural clients who came in. Ever since the Big Uneasy, the celestial event that returned all the monsters and magic to the normal world, I had offered my services to clients, both human and inhuman.

The werewolf woman snorted, sobbed, and blew her nose again. She dropped the sodden, tattered tissues on Sheyenne's desk. "My name is Myra Blankenship. My son Aldo is missing! Please help me find him, Mr. Shamble."

I don't know why I bother correcting the pronunciation anymore, but it's automatic. "The name is *Chambeaux*, Ms. Blankenship. Tell me what happened."

My lawyer partner, Robin Deyer, emerged from her own office on the other side of the conference room. She's a fiery African-American attorney who wants justice for all unnaturals. She held a yellow legal pad and a pencil, both of which were spell-bonded, so they took notes all by themselves. "I heard growling." She paused, spotting the distraught werewolf. "How can we help you, ma'am?" Robin has a huge heart and a stubborn spirit. Without even hearing Myra's story, she immediately added, "We'll put the full resources of Chambeaux and Deyer on the case."

"It's gang related," said Myra. She rummaged in her small clutch purse and withdrew a photo of her son.

Aldo was a string bean, nerdy-looking werewolf kid about fourteen years old. He had a bad furry haircut, horn-rimmed glasses, and a red plaid shirt that was obviously a hand-me-down. His smile showed braces on his fangs.

"Aldo was a good boy, but he fell in with a bad crowd. He wanted to join a gang, so he could feel tough." She sniffled and sobbed, then rubbed her paws across her facial fur, which only served to smear the snot and tears around. Her mascara ran down among the brown strands of fur. "I told him to get good grades in school, but I don't know where I went wrong. He had no business hanging out with hoodlum genies. We're not even from the same mythologies!"

Sheyenne drifted forward to hand Myra a glass of water from the tap in our little kitchenette.

Myra continued as her explanation swiftly built into a howl. "It's ... it's been difficult at home. Aldo's father and I are getting a—" Her voice hitched. "A divorce. And it hit the poor boy hard. He's just acting out, but I'm sure he's in deep trouble. Now he's *gone*! *Arrooooooo*!"

Sheyenne brought forth a clipboard with our new client form while Robin stood listening as her pencil took detailed notes on the legal pad.

I said, "Once we have all the background, ma'am, I'll start looking for your Aldo right away. I assure you, this is my most important case." It was my only active case, but I like to make the client feel good.

I listened intently as Myra Blankenship rattled off

details about her son and his presumed predicament, but like many werewolf parents—or parents of any species— she knew little about her son's after-school activities.

When she had told me everything, I donned my sport jacket with the stitched-up bullet holes and settled my fedora in place, tilting it forward to hide the bullet hole in my forehead. "That's enough for me to start with, ma'am. Don't you worry. I'll find your son." I squared my shoulders and tucked my .38 in my side pocket. "Hoodlum genies don't bother me one bit."

II

The Unnatural Quarter is a colorful, bustling, and interesting place that looks like any other large downtown, but with a difference: much of the population consists of monsters of various kinds. But monsters still have jobs, still go shopping, still hail cabs, still get into fights, and still have personal problems like everybody else.

I passed a blood bar where two classic-looking Bela Lugosi-style vampires sat under a black awning, chatting away and sipping at red, frothy blood plasmaccinos. A sandwich board in front of the door read, "Special Today, double shots of B-positive." Someone had scrawled a smiley face beneath it.

A black-furred werewolf tightened the strings on his apron and worked outside of his little shop, setting out packages of steaks in the butcher's display case. A tattered, half-unraveled mummy sat in a rickety canvas chair in front of a newspaper stand. Some of the newspapers were printed on papyrus in hieroglyphics, while other papers were more traditional next to a colorful display of magazines. One of the more prominent periodicals was *People*, and next to it was a similar magazine called *Monsters*. An alligator man in a business suit and tie stood at the magazine rack, thumbing through that week's copy of *Monsters*.

I love this place.

Everybody knows the magical explanation for the Big Uneasy, when all the legendary creatures returned to the world about ten years ago: a rare planetary alignment, a full moon, spilled virgin's blood, a cursed spell book, human clumsiness ... you know, the usual. All the vampires, werewolves, ghosts, zombies, mummies, and demons caused quite an uproar for a while, but, when you get down to it, monsters just want to live a normal life like anyone else.

I strolled along the sidewalk, smelling the smells (not all of them terrible), seeing the sights, watching the people. As a detective, I absorb details, never knowing what might become useful. Today I kept my eyes open for clues about the missing werewolf kid. I needed to start somewhere.

How hard could it be to find a gang of delinquent genies?

On the sidewalk ahead, I saw a beat cop in his traditional blue uniform with a cap covering his dark red hair. When he saw me, his freckled face lit up in a grin that seemed deceptively friendly. Officer Toby McGoohan is indeed my Best Human Friend, but his friendly smile usually comes with consequences. He raised his hand in greeting as I came up to him. "Hey, Shamble! I've got one for you." His expression became more eager, like a predator about to pounce. "What comes out of a ghost's nose when he sneezes?"

"I don't suppose there's any way I can talk you out of finishing the joke?"

McGoo cackled. "BOO-gers. Get it? *BOO*-gers. Ha, ha!"

"Hasn't your sense of humor already gotten you into enough trouble? You should learn your lesson."

"Some lessons can't be taught." He placed his hands on his hips near his police special revolver and in the opposite holster his police extra-special revolver loaded with silver bullets.

"I don't have any time for jokes, McGoo. I'm on a case. I've been hired to track down a missing teenage werewolf. His mom says he hung out with a gang of low-life genies. Any idea where I should start to look?"

McGoo frowned. "Low-life genies? Might be the Baba brothers. Genies are usually high-class, but these boys are scum."

"The Baba brothers?" I asked.

McGoo nodded. "Bill, Joe, and Frank Baba. They have their own territory. It's an alley down in the Undertakers' District." He looked up, alert as he watched a full-furred werewolf amble up to a fire hydrant, then bend over, sniffing it.

I adjusted my fedora. "I know where that is. Thanks, McGoo."

Ignoring me, he yelled, "Hey you, Wolfie! Don't you dare lift your leg by that fire hydrant."

Indignant, the wolf straightened and tried to be

nonchalant. "I'm just looking for a friend." He scuttled off while I headed in the other direction, toward the Undertakers' District.

III

Even though I knew the Unnatural Quarter like the back of my cold, gray hand, the maze of narrow side streets and tangled back alleys is a labyrinth that even a minotaur could get lost in. I got so turned around that I had to ask for directions, despite being male.

Finally, by late afternoon, I stumbled upon my destination, isolated turf that the three Baba brothers had claimed as their territory. It was unofficially known as the Alley Baba.

As I turned the corner and shambled forward, I heard voices shouting, the rattle of dice in a cup, and the clatter as they ricocheted off the brick walls. "Come on sevens! Come on sevens!"

I saw the three genies, seedy-looking teens, their skin and silk garments glowing as they drifted off the ground. They wore colorful green pantaloons, their heads wrapped in identical scarlet turbans, which I knew were gang colors in the Quarter. Frank Baba, the oldest, lounged against a brick wall wearing a big, diamond-studded belt buckle that would have been the envy of any wrestler or country-and-western fan. Another genie—Joe—sneered down at the corner watching the dice clatter. The third and youngest genie crouched but floated just enough off the ground to keep his silk pantaloons from getting dirty in the grunge of the alley. Bill Baba rolled the dice again, chuckling. "Come on sevens! Come on!"

The pair of twenty-sided D-and-D dice rattled and came to rest, facing up, each showing the number seven. Bill let out a loud whoop. "Yesssss! Sevens! I win every time."

Lounging against the wall, his brother Frank just sneered at him. "It's not much of a game when all your wishes come true, Bill."

I shuffled forward. "Hey, fellas." I like to begin a conversation by showing I'm a friendly zombie and not one of the violent brain-eating types. "I could use your help, if you've got time for a few questions?"

The three genies swooped toward me like weightless thugs about to mug a pedestrian. Unobtrusively, I slipped my hand into my jacket pocket where I kept my .38. Before I was forced to exercise my second amendment rights, I realized the genies were all bluster.

"Why should we help you?" demanded Frank Baba. "Just cuz we're genies doesn't mean you can command us."

"I wish I could," I said.

"Don't say that!" he cried.

"Yeah," said Bill, "and if you try to rub my lamp, I'll slap your hand."

"We're busy," Joe sneered. "We have a lot of slacking to do, and only so many hours in the day."

I used the pause as an opportunity to continue. "I've been hired to locate a friend of yours, Aldo Blankenship. I understand you hang out together?"

The three genies chortled in unison. Their combined laughter sounded like an odd hybrid of a bagpipe and a popcorn popper. Joe laughed so hard that he did a spinning backward barrel roll in the air. "Aldo? A *friend* of ours? That kid was just a useless wanna-be."

"Right," said Bill. "A whiny werewolf brat."

"He wasn't cut out to be one of us," Frank said. "We tolerated him because we needed his smarts for a job, that's all."

Joe put his glowing face close to mine. Despite his magical properties, the young genie suffered from a severe case of acne. "Aldo was miserable about his parents splitting up. He came to us pouting, grumbling. He said he wished the world would just get back to normal. Ha, ha!" His face pinched up in an utterly humorless expression. "Back to normal! When you're talking to genies, you better be careful what you wish for!"

Very little seemed normal about the situation, and I gave all three of the genies my best stern look. "Well, *I* wish I could find Aldo and close my case. You guys know where I should start looking? Give me a hint."

Slacker hoodlum genie teenagers have no poker face whatsoever, which was probably why they played dice instead of cards. "We had work to do, so we sent Aldo on an errand. He helped us out." Bill looked meaningfully at the bricked-up end of Alley Baba, where a battered red metal toolbox leaned against the solid wall. I didn't know what the toolbox had to do with anything.

"But I don't think the kid's coming back," said Frank.

The genies had that guilty look any good detective can recognize immediately.

I crossed my arms over my chest just above the stitched-up bullet holes on my jacket. "You boys better start explaining yourselves. What happened to Aldo?"

Bill shrugged.

Joe adjusted the scarlet turban on his head. "It was an initiation and … it kinda went sour."

Frank nodded. "Aldo opened a portal for us back to the mundane world, right here at the end of the alley. He wished for things to be normal, and we needed a portal anyway."

"The kid went through the doorway back to the normal world, and he never came back." Joe hovered over the red metal toolbox on the ground.

I was still trying to understand what had happened. "A dimensional portal? How did Aldo manage to create a portal?"

"It's easy, if you know how," said Frank.

"You can do anything when you have the right tools." Joe seemed eager to explain, because criminals often do. "And we just happen to have this arcane toolbox."

I bent down, flipped open the latch and lifted the lid, but the box was mostly empty, with only a flashlight and a measuring tape inside. I picked up the flashlight and saw mysterious runes printed on its handle. I realized the three genies looked worried. Bill continued, "Each tool has magical runes on it, a transport spell written in original Necronomic. But we, uh …"

Frank added, "We couldn't read them ourselves. We

missed that day in class because we were out smoking behind the school."

"So we needed Aldo to read the runes for us," Bill said. "We're not too good at reading, especially in arcane Necronomic."

Frank grumbled, "Now Aldo's lost on the other side, and we can't open the portals anymore."

The case wasn't much of a mystery, since the three genie brothers had babbled everything, but I still didn't know what they were talking about. Aldo had wished for things to be back to normal, and he used that power plus these magical tools to open up a dimensional gateway to the normal world? For what?

And what was normal anymore?

I also knew these slacker genies could never have cooked up such a scheme all by themselves. "Who put you up to this? Who else knows how to open a portal to the mundane world?"

The genies hesitated, looked at one another as if daring someone to be first to answer. Finally, they spoke in unison. "You have to talk to Vlad the Fence."

IV

Over the years, I've had a few encounters with Vlad the Fence, mostly at cocktail parties and ice cream socials. Vlad was one of the most infamous "liquidators" of stolen artifacts in the Quarter, but then he claimed he was going straight. Don't they all say that?

I found the ramshackle storefront with a patched, gray-striped awning and a crackling neon sign that said *High Stakes Pawn Shop*. The narrow, dingy street was silent except for water dripping from gutters above. The dark alley had very little foot traffic and even fewer customers, which was probably the reason for the prominent "GOING OUT OF BUSINESS" sign hanging in the window.

I shoved open the door, and a delicate jingling bell announced my arrival. The shop was small and cramped, cluttered with more empty shelves than esoteric objects. Most of the inventory had either been sold or packed up. It was disappointing to see how far Vlad had fallen, because he used to be somebody, a powerful legendary figure who called himself "The Impaler," like a Mexican wrestling superstar. But unlife hadn't treated him well.

"Hello?" I called into the dark shadows. "Vlad! I need some information from you."

In the back of the poorly lit shop, a figure let out a startled gasp. In a panic, Vlad the Fence dropped a cardboard box that crashed to the floor, then slapped his palm to his chest, gasping. "Whoa, drive a stake right through my heart, why don't you?"

I tried to calm him. "Just because a zombie barges through your front door, there's no need to be afraid. I'm sure you've had worse customers."

He let out a sigh of relief as he recognized me. "Dan Shamble! Trouble follows you wherever you go."

"It's usually a few steps ahead of me," I said. "I don't go looking for it."

Vlad had long, scraggly black hair, a narrow, pale face, a sinister mustache, and now he had bags under his eyes.

He groaned at the clutter that had spilled out of the cardboard box he'd been packing. He dropped to his knees, embarrassed, and started to pick up the paraphernalia, spiked manacles, petrified claws, antique Pez dispensers.

Numerous cardboard moving boxes were scattered throughout the shop, some open and half-packed, others taped up. I stepped closer to him, all business. "I just have a few questions about a case and then I'll be out of your hair."

Vlad finished stuffing the odds and ends back into the box and folded the four corners together, trying to figure out which order the up corner went amongst the down corners. "Can't help you. I'm out of the business. Packing up and changing professions."

"Are you going to have a garage sale?" I asked. "Or just donate all this junk to a charity?"

"Some of it is just junk, but other pieces ..." Vlad stroked his long mustache and cleared his throat. "They're dangerous and have to be disposed of properly." He gestured to a secure, heavy-duty showcase cabinet in the back corner. It had a thick crossbar and latch, wrapped with barbed wire. Big signs were posted on each side. "DANGER. DO NOT ENTER. HAZARDOUS MAGICAL MATERIALS."

"No special sale would get rid of those, and the liability is too much for me to handle," Vlad said. "I did manage to liquidate the cursed artifacts, the bad luck gems, the Skull of Synthnoxx. It's all gone, so I'm clean." He stood up again, still panicked and nervous. "You've got nothing on me, Shamble. I'm just trying to make a living, even though

I'm going out of business." He shook his head, making his oily, black strands of hair flop back and forth like tentacles. "I would've thought a magical pawn shop was a recession-proof business, but times are tough, and I can't afford the insurance anymore." He chuckled to himself as he dropped the repacked box next to others on a shelf. "That's where the real money is—insurance."

"Insurance?" I asked.

Vlad's shoulders sagged. "But even that's complicated. How do you even write a policy for undead and unnaturals, and what do you cover? When can you accept a claim? I wish the world would go back to normal."

I nodded in polite commiseration, but then I realized the werewolf kid had supposedly said the same thing.

Vlad was caught up in his indignant nostalgia. His chest puffed up, his shoulders squared, and his voice grew louder, deeper. "I used to be Vlad the Impaler, and armies trembled before me. I had five castles, countless women, dungeons full of gold!" He sighed. "Now, I can't even make ends meet as Vlad the Fence. So, I'm retiring, to become Vlad the Insurance Salesman." He deflated as he realized what he had said. "Yeah, times are tough."

"We have our jobs to do." I reached into the pocket of my jacket and withdrew the photo of the young werewolf with his bad fur cut, his glasses, the braces on his fangs. "I've been hired to find a missing boy."

Vlad squinted, leaning closer in the dim light of the High Stakes pawn shop. "Never seen him before." It sounded like an automatic response, and when I appeared to disbelieve him, he shook his head more insistently.

"Honest, Shamble. Why would you think I have anything to do with it?" Vlad stuffed a couple of skulls into another box, packing them with Styrofoam peanuts.

"He got himself mixed up with some disreputable genies, the Baba brothers," I said. "They're the ones who pointed me to you."

When I mentioned the genies, Vlad glared at me. "The Babas are a bad crowd." He sighed. "But I needed their help. You know the saying, hire bad people to do bad work."

"I've never heard that saying," I said.

Vlad left the skulls and the Styrofoam peanuts, heading to the cabinet of dangerous items. He pried aside the barbed wire and pulled the door open to reveal that the cabinet was entirely empty. "As I said, I'm shutting down the business, and I had to liquidate the dangerous items. I didn't dare keep them around—insurance rates, remember? A liability!" He reached inside, pulled out a hand-written inventory list. "You know, things like the Scroll of Vileness, the Balls of Testic, the Amulet of Apathy, the real high-end stuff." He shut the metal door again with a loud clang. "So I paid the Baba brothers to get rid of the toxic artifacts." He pointed a long finger at me. "We didn't dare leave them in the Unnatural Quarter, so I told the Babas they had to dump them somewhere else. I gave them the tools they needed to get the job done."

"Tools?" I asked. "Like a skill set?"

Vlad went back to closing up the cardboard flaps over the preserved skulls. "No, actual *magical tools*, a toolbox full of ensorcelled hammers, wrenches, screwdrivers, tape measures. Each tool could open a portal back to the mundane world, an alternate Earth where the Big Uneasy never happened, and where magic doesn't work."

That sounded doubtful to me. "I didn't know that was possible."

"You don't believe in alternate dimensions?" Vlad said. "Don't you read the *Enquirer*?"

I shrugged. "I'll take your word for it. These days it's not smart to disbelieve any ridiculous thing."

"In order to open the portal, you have to read the engraved spell on the tool," Vlad said. "It's written in complex runes, and each tool only works once. You use it and throw it away."

I found that disturbing. "Everything's disposable nowadays."

Vlad extended his other hand and pointed a different long finger at me. This one had blue nail polish. "The Baba brothers had the whole toolbox so they could open portals to a parallel universe, and they did the job—I'll give them that. They got rid of all those Items That Shall Not Be Named."

"Items That Shall Not Be Named? You hired the Baba brothers to dispose of your unmentionables?"

Vlad bustled around the pawn shop, using a tape gun to reinforce more cardboard boxes, then stuffed them with odds and ends from the near empty shelves. He kept busy as he talked. "Frankly, I'm surprised those screwups could handle the job. You have to read the incantation exactly right." He sniffed. "I was surprised they could read at all."

Now the pieces began to fit together in my mind.

"Hmm, that's why they needed Aldo's help. He was a straight-A student and he knew how to read. He used the spells to open the portals, and he somehow got stranded on the wrong side after the doorway closed. Now I need to use one of those tools to get Aldo back." I could just imagine how the three hoodlum genies had tricked the innocent little kid. "What's the incantation?"

Vlad closed his eyes and recited something that sounded like a slurring drunk played backward. "*Rutmo byachto seengac igsnat.* It means 'there's no place like home,' in Necronomic. Pronunciation is very important."

"That sounds hard to remember," I said.

"Not if you can read the Necronomic runes on the tools." He tore a scrap of paper from a battered Egyptian scroll and scribbled a note on the papyrus. "Here, I've written it down for you phonetically."

V

Back in Alley Baba, the three hoodlum genies were at it again, cheering each other as Frank rattled the twenty-sided dice in his hands. He cast them against the slimy brick wall. "Come on, sevens!"

The dice bounced and rolled, scattering a group of panicked cockroaches who were just minding their own business in the rotting garbage. The genies whooped in triumph. "Sevens, yes!" The Baba brothers high-fived each other.

"It's your lucky day in more ways than one, boys," I said, trying to sound ominous as I approached. "But you've got some explaining to do. I talked with Vlad the Fence, and I know what happened to that poor werewolf kid. Aldo wanted to be part of your gang, and you needed someone who could read Necronomic to work the spells on the tools." I saw the battered magical tool chest lying on the ground against the brick wall.

"The kid was always hanging around, very needy," said Joe. "He wanted to be tough, so we gave him something to do. Made him useful."

"We needed to get rid of those dangerous artifacts," said Bill. "It was ... yeah, a *community service*. And we've done community service plenty of times before."

Frank retrieved the twenty-sided dice from the ground. "That werewolf kid was smart. He could read the runes."

Joe shuffled his feet even though he was drifting a few inches off the ground. "He wanted to be part of the gang, so we had to initiate him. After we got rid of the other magical junk and used up most of the tools, we made him jump through when he opened the last portal. He was supposed to come right back." He grumbled. "But the stupid furball moved too slow, and the portal closed before he could come home."

Frowning, I used my forefinger to scratch around the bullet hole in my forehead. "So, he's stranded in the mundane world."

"But he should have been able to come back all by himself," Bill said. "He still had one of the unused tools. I think it was a pair of scissors."

I went to the toolbox and lifted the metal lid, saw the two tools remaining, a flashlight and a measuring tape, both of them covered with runes. "When he didn't come back right away, you just left him there. Why didn't you open another portal so he could return?"

The genies were embarrassed. "We couldn't read the runes. That was our problem in the first place."

"Yeah," Bill said. "The spell is really hard to remember. Who talks like that anyway?"

If the genies were really genies, they should have been able to wish a portal into existence. Intellectually speaking, their lamps seemed rather dim.

In my pocket, I felt the scrap of paper Vlad had given me. It would be up to me to open a portal and fetch Aldo back from the "real world," safe and sound, just as his mother had hired me to do. I picked up the rune-etched flashlight, slammed the toolbox lid and lifted it by the handle. "I've got to rescue the kid, and I'm taking the toolbox with me, before you mess anything up again."

The genies were happy to let me do the spellcasting and rune reading. Gripping the toolbox handle, I held the flashlight in my other hand along with the strip of paper and the phonetic pronunciation. I faced the brick wall, cleared my throat, and pronounced the incantation. *"Rutmo byachto seengac igsnat."*

The flashlight thrummed and throbbed. I watched it glow, but the real special-effects budget was spent on the wall itself. The bricks shimmered, and a glowing blue whirlpool appeared. A spectacular portal opened up, framed with lighting, something Lucasfilm only wished they could do.

"Whoa!" I said, hoping that wouldn't disrupt the spell.

Through the shimmering doorway I could see another alley, remarkably similar to this one, but it was nighttime there. Aldo Blankenship was on the other side, and I had to retrieve him. Without wasting time on an actual plan, I stepped through.

My gut twisted as I plunged into the ripple, but it was probably indigestion or anxiety, rather than the after-effect of dimensional transport. A *whoosh* roared in my ears as I stepped through into another world, a place much like the Unnatural Quarter, but with nothing unnatural about it, where the Big Uneasy had never happened, a place suitable for the disposal of toxic magical artifacts.

A world where real zombies and real werewolves were definitely not welcome.

There's no place like home.

VI

With unsettling abruptness, the portal whisked shut behind me. The glowing special effects dwindled, leaving me with only a brick wall behind me. It was dark, late at night, so time must be different in this other world. I was stranded.

Here on the other side of the doorway, I saw odd debris strewn among the garbage in the dark alley. Broken lizard eggs, a demon skull missing one horn, a cursed letter opener, an obsidian-encrusted flyswatter, and other weird artifacts, permanently deactivated in the mundane world and suitable for nothing more than the last-pick items in a white elephant sale.

But Aldo wasn't here. Monsters or not, this was undoubtedly a big city, and I had no idea where the werewolf kid might have wandered in the few days he'd been stranded here. I doubted Aldo was clever or sneaky. Where would he have slept? What would he eat? Poor Aldo must have been so frightened, hiding in shadows, rummaging in dumpsters, huddled under flattened cardboard.

I heard traffic out in the main streets, cars honking, the bustle of city life. No one seemed to be on the dark side street, not even muggers or derelicts. No sign of Aldo, though.

As a good boy, he probably would have thought to go directly to the police station, but what would they do with a furry-faced teenager with glasses and braces?

A werewolf on the loose, even a nerdy one, must have caused some kind of an uproar in a normal world. I'd have to use all my skills as a detective to track down sightings of a monster boy. Alas, the fact that I was a zombie myself would make things difficult. The bullet hole in my forehead would distract them. But I was determined. I had to start somewhere, and I knew I had a long search ahead of me.

Or maybe not. Though I always insist it isn't so, sometimes the cases really do solve themselves. I suddenly heard wailing police sirens, five or six cop cars racing straight toward my alley.

Panting hard, a suspect bolted around the corner and dashed headlong into the alley. I saw his furry face, his glasses, the braces prominent on his fangs as he let his tongue loll out. He bounded along at full speed, holding a pair of scissors in his paw. I wanted to warn him about running with scissors, that he might poke someone's eye out, and then I realized these were the rune-etched scissors.

Terrified, Aldo Blankenship bleated as he ran, reading from the runes on the scissors, barking out the spell again and again. *"Rutmo byachtu seengac igsnot! Rutmo byachtu seengac igsnot! Rutmo byachtu seengac igsnot!"*

"Aldo!" I waved vigorously to get his attention. "Aldo Blankenship! I'm here to save you!"

"Thank heavens," he gasped, scrambling toward me as the police sirens closed in. "A zombie to the rescue."

"Your mother sent me to find you," I said, reaching toward him. "She's worried sick."

Aldo nearly burst into tears. "I've been trying to get back home. I read the spell over and over again." He waved the scissors in the air, and I backed away to a safe distance. "This was my spare tool. I should've been able to get home. But it doesn't work!" He poked the scissors too close to my face.

"Careful," I said.

"Now the cops are after me. I was so hungry, I shoplifted some pastrami from a deli. I tried to be sneaky, but everyone kept staring at me," Aldo said. "Maybe because I was the only werewolf in the shop."

"You're the only werewolf in the whole world," I said. "And I'm the only zombie. We've got to get out of here."

The sirens grew louder. The flashlight in my hand had ceased glowing after the portal closed, and now it wouldn't even turn on a normal beam when I flipped the power switch. I realized that nobody had put batteries inside. "This one's used up."

Aldo waved the scissors again. "I haven't used these yet." He stared at the runes. "I'm reading the spell, word for word, but isn't working. *Rutmo byachtu seengac igsnot!*"

I took out my phonetic pronunciation spell and frowned. "You're not saying it right. Look here, it should be *byachto* instead of *byachtu* and *igsnat* instead of *igsnot*."

Aldo groaned. "There's a typo on my scissors! It won't work. The spell is defective."

"I guess you could call it a real mis*spell*ing." I set the metal toolbox on the ground, flipped the latch, and pulled out the measuring tape, the last tool in the set. "We have one more chance. We'll use this to open the portal back to the Unnatural Quarter and get safely home."

I heard screeching tires, the wailing of sirens, shouted voices, and crackling police radios. "Hurry!" Aldo cried. "I can't go to jail!"

I held up the measuring tape, pulled it out to twelve inches, just to be sure it was properly loaded. The numbers on the tape were unreadable and unpronounceable runes, but I had my phonetic cheat sheet.

I hadn't been here long. Part of me thought wistfully about the chance to wander through the mundane world again, the *normal* world. The good old days without magic, ghosts, monsters, or toxic arcane items. But back in that world, if I'd been killed on a case, I would have stayed dead, and so would my girlfriend Sheyenne.

I realized I would miss my Unnatural Quarter, my favorite hangouts like the Ghoul's Diner and the Goblin

Tavern. I'd miss the werewolves and vampires, the unraveling mummies, the mischievous lawn gnomes. I would miss my partner, Robin, and my Best Human Friend, McGoo. And I never wanted to be separated from Sheyenne again, 'til death do us part and then some.

"Come on, kid, we're going home." I held up the measuring tape as we ran back toward the brick wall.

I heard footsteps and shouts, silhouetted figures of cops running in from the main street, flashing blue and red light splashed at the mouth of the alley. "Hey, you! Stop right there!"

I replied with, *"Rutmo byachto seengac igsnat."*

Just like before, a sequel to the first movie but with an even bigger special-effects budget, the wall shimmered and glowed as a dimensional doorway appeared. Looking through to the other side, we could see daylight and the Baba brothers staring at us, mouths open, eyes wide.

"They waited for me!" Aldo said. "Look, my gang is there for me."

"They're not your gang, kid."

Behind us, the cops yelled louder, guns drawn as they ran from their squad cars. They hadn't even seen that we were a werewolf and a zombie yet, but they sure seemed angry about the stolen pastrami.

I grabbed Aldo by the scrawny arm and yanked him with me. I still held the now-empty tool kit as we plunged into the portal, whisked from the mundane world to the Unnatural Quarter again, a place where monsters could be safe.

The portal closed behind us with an audible pop and a burst of fireworks.

I was surprised to see McGoo standing there with a stern look on his face and a threatening finger jabbing at the air as he lectured the cowed genie brothers. He must have been getting up to full steam when the portal opened.

Vlad the Fence also stood there, looking very worried, but he brightened when he saw me stumble back through the doorway, teenaged werewolf in tow. "See, I told you! And he's got the toolbox, too."

"It's empty now," I said, holding up the red-painted box. "I had to use the measuring tape to get home, so the mundane world is safely separated from us. The monsters are safe now."

"And all of the dangerous artifacts are gone, safely disposed of," Vlad said, grinning nervously. "See, Officer McGoohan, I told you we'd get your friend back. And the Unnatural Quarter is free of toxic sorcerous knickknacks."

"Yeah," said Frank Baba in a huff. "We made it safe. It's our community service."

McGoo stepped to the brick wall and pounded on it with his fist. "Yeah, closed up tight as a sphincter. No leaks."

I faced the three surly-looking genies, the young were-wolf next to me, then glanced out into the streets, which were filled with ghosts, frog demons, mummies, slithering things, and looming things—exactly the Unnatural Quarter I remembered.

Aldo sniffled, miserable and shaken. Tears made tracks

down his furry face. I clapped my hand on his shoulder. "You need to get a new circle of friends, kid."

"I'm not a kid," Aldo snapped. "I want my mommy."

VII

The Blankenship house was a painfully normal suburban home, a three-bedroom ranch model like something out of a 1960s sitcom from the mundane world. Maybe it, too, had been whisked through a portal and landed here.

With such a heartwarming wrap-up to a case, I couldn't wait to see the look of joy on the furry werewolf faces. As I escorted Aldo home, I still carried the empty toolbox, though I didn't know what I'd ever use it for. Maybe a souvenir of successful detective work.

Aldo loped ahead to the front door, howling. "Mom! Mom, I'm home!"

Myra Blankenship burst out onto the porch full of joy, opening her furry arms to embrace her son. "Aldo! We were so worried about you."

Next to her came a burly, middle-aged werewolf man with a buzzcut, wearing a work shirt and jeans, a typical blue-collar werewolf. He growled, "Glad to see you back, son, safe and sound."

"Dad?" Aldo yelped. "Dad! What are you doing here? I thought you and mom split up."

The two adult werewolves looked at each other, and deep feelings passed between their canine eyes. Together, they swept Aldo into a furry group hug. The scene was wonderfully sappy and clichéd, but I wouldn't have changed it for anything. I kept my distance, just looming there on the sidewalk holding the empty toolbox.

Mr. Blankenship explained, "When you were gone, son, I realized all the things I missed about home. Your mother and I have decided to try to work it out."

Myra squeezed her son even tighter, wrapping her other arm around her husband's waist. "We'll be a real family again."

I waited there, enjoying the Hallmark moment. It would have been heartwarming, if I had a heart that still worked. For a zombie detective, one of the most gratifying moments is when I can say the words *Case Closed.*

And then Sheyenne can send out the bill.

VIII

Just when I thought it was safe to go back to the office.

Having wrapped up the missing werewolf case, I went back to ignore paperwork. I sat in my office, looking at the manila folders of a few pending, but uninteresting cases. I put my shoes up on the desk, leaned back in my office chair to the comforting creaks and groans of the springs.

Sheyenne kept the empty toolbox on her desk, trying to figure out where to store it. I'm not much of a handyman, since I'm better at breaking things instead of fixing them.

McGoo popped in to say hello, as he usually did when he wanted to avoid walking the beat. "Those three Baba brothers are trouble," he grinned. "But they're *in* trouble now. They crossed a line with poor Aldo Blankenship. Bill and Joe are under age, but we did arrest Frank for disposing of dangerous magical artifacts without a license. He'll use up his three wishes he has on a phone call, extra time in the yard, and packs of cigarettes in prison. No doubt he'll be sentenced to serve ten to fifteen years in a lamp."

I came out to greet him. "I've never been a fan of juvenile delinquents. You meeting me at the Goblin Tavern tonight?"

He raised his eyebrows. "Are you asking me out on a date, Shamble?"

"He's taken," Sheyenne said, smiling. "But I'll let him have a beer with you."

We were all relaxing in the calm after-case glow, and then Vlad the Fence kicked open the door to our offices, on the verge of destroying the world. He barged in, his dark eyes wide, his scraggly hair dangling in front of his wild expression. He dragged the young genie Bill Baba by the glowing ear. "I need your help or it'll be the end of everything!"

In his other hand Vlad carried a nasty-looking talisman that looked like it came from some old grandma's rummage sale. It was ceramic, bulbous, a cross between an ashtray and a dog food dish. And it was *smoking*.

Bill struggled and flailed. "I didn't do it. I didn't do it!"

"Right this way, Bill Baba." Vlad flung the genie in front of McGoo and me. "You better hope we can fix this." Furious, he held up the smoking, burbling talisman which gave off anything but good vibrations.

"What is it, Vlad? What did the genies do now?" I asked. McGoo was ready with his handcuffs.

Vlad looked as if he wanted to tear Bill Baba limb from limb. "Those numbskull genies kept one of the most dangerous arcane artifacts they were supposed to dispose of!" He held up the ashtray / dog food dish. "The Talisman of Terribleness. It's practically radioactive with sorcery, and now this idiot triggered it."

"I was trying to light a cigarette," Bill mumbled. "I didn't know what it was. I just found it there."

McGoo looked at the throbbing, toxic artifact. "That sounds bad. Really bad."

"Like end-of-the-world bad," I said.

"We were going to sell it on eBay," Bill cried. "Joe and I needed extra cash, now that Frank is arrested."

Vlad dropped the Talisman of Terribleness on Sheyenne's desk. "It's the last of the dangerous relics from my vault. We have to get rid of it."

Sheyenne frowned in dismay at the smoking, sizzling relic scorching the wood on her desk. "Careful with the surface. That's solid oak."

The terrified genie babbled, "I wish I could get out of here!"

Then in a self-fulfilling manner, he vanished with a popping sound in the air. We all looked in shock at where he had disappeared, leaving the surging, deadly artifact behind.

Vlad groaned deep in his throat, and his shoulders slumped in defeat. "I just wanted to retire and sell insurance. I wanted everything to be normal."

McGoo looked at me, then at Vlad. "How do we stop it? Can we dump it in a bucket of water or something? How much time do we have left?"

Vlad was terrified. "I don't know!"

I said, "Is there a counter spell? Some kind of toxic magic disposal? A sorcerous disinfectant?"

"The only way to get rid of it is to open a portal and send it to the mundane world where the magic is neutralized." He saw the red toolbox on the desk. "And you used up all the tools! We don't have anything left, no way to open a portal." He slumped into the guest chair. "I am so tired of this nonsense. I just wanted to go straight. Now it's the end of the world."

Robin came out to see what all the commotion was, but since even such emergencies were common occurrences in the Chambeaux & Deyer offices, she assumed we had it all under control and went back to work on a new legal brief.

I opened the magical toolbox on the corner of the desk, hoping against hope there might be some arcane paper clip or screw unnoticed in the corner. But it was truly empty, nothing but the toolbox itself.

The Talisman of Terribleness throbbed brighter, hotter, nastier, ready to explode.

In hopeless disgust, I slammed the lid shut again and tipped over the box. Suddenly, I saw runes on the bottom, the same strange incantation that I had seen engraved on the flashlight, the screwdriver, and the scissors (except for the small typographical error). "Oh! The toolbox is part of the set, too."

Vlad gasped and brightened. "Of course it is! Why

didn't I think of that? We used all the tools, but the box itself is the last item."

Fortunately, I still had the phonetic pronunciation—and no time to lose. I would read the Necronomic runes and open a portal. "Let's dump this relic into the normal world!"

"A place where the magic won't work, a place without monsters," Vlad said, sounding wistful. "A place where people can just be normal again."

The Talisman continued smoking on Sheyenne's desk, more ominous than ever. Even though I often can't remember my own phone number, or my street address— nothing to do with the bullet hole in my head, just distracted—I rattled off the magical words. *"Rutmo byachto seengac igsnat."*

Right there in the middle of the office, next to the plastic potted plant, a spectacular special-effects portal opened in the air, glowing even brighter than the radioactive Talisman of Terribleness ready to erupt on Sheyenne's desk. I lurched for the artifact so I could throw it through the doorway.

But Vlad got there first. With a determined look on his face, he grabbed the Talisman and wrapped his arms around it as he spun to the portal. "The magic won't work there, so I'll be safe. I can be a normal insurance salesman—just the way I always wanted to be."

"Wait, it's a one-way trip," I cried. "You'll never be able to come back to the Unnatural Quarter."

"That's the idea," said Vlad the Fence. He jumped

through the shimmering dimensional doorway. "Too damn many curses back here."

I threw the magical toolbox after him for good measure, and I just missed his head, but I didn't want the thing around here at all. Maybe Vlad could use it, to store a set of mundane tools, if nothing else. The portal slammed shut with a vacuum pop, and the dangerous magic dissipated around us.

Everything was back to our own version of normal.

Sheyenne frowned at the scorch mark on her desk, then strategically placed a stack of unpaid invoices on top of it, which satisfied her.

McGoo removed his cap and wiped sweat from his forehead. "Yes, I'll take you up on that beer later tonight, Shamble."

"Why does it have to be later?" I asked. "I could use one now."

Since it was late in the afternoon, we left the office and headed out into the streets of the Quarter, making our way to the Goblin Tavern. I looked around at the familiar street scene filled with everyday monsters. A witch in a pointy black hat stood arguing with an ogre beside two cars caught in a fender-bender, each of them yelling at each other and exchanging insurance numbers. Another monster strolled by, pushing a baby carriage. A boy mummy zipped along on a skateboard, performing dangerous tricks that could easily snap his ancient bones or tear some of his bandages.

I found it all comforting. More than a decade after the Big Uneasy, I'd grown used to this. I understood the rules and my place, and I was a damn good detective, zombie or otherwise. I silently wished Vlad the best, knowing he would make a very good insurance salesman back in the mundane world.

But this place was normal to me now, and I certainly wouldn't wish for anything else.

Game Night

Chambeaux & Deyer Investigations was not a place for fun and games. As a zombie detective, I take my cases seriously. Some clients might even say dead seriously—and only half of them would be making a stupid joke.

My human partner, Robin Deyer, is a practicing attorney with a heart of gold, determined to see justice for all the monsters who had returned to the world a decade ago. We each had a full caseload to keep ourselves busy: werewolves still got divorced, mad scientists sued each other for patent infringements, ghosts vanished without meeting their financial obligations, mummies still watched their business dealings unravel.

Some cases were dangerous, and that's how I'd ended up shot dead in an alley after getting too close to an evil criminal mastermind. No one was more surprised than me when I woke up as a zombie, dug myself out of the grave, and got back to work on my cases.

No, we didn't have time for fun and games—at least not usually.

Sheyenne, my beautiful blond-haired, blue-eyed ghost girlfriend drifted up to me as I stared at a pile of unsolved case folders on my desk. I hoped, without success, for some important clue to jump out at me like an inconvenient cat from the shadows in a low-budget horror movie.

It was long after dark in the Unnatural Quarter, but the dead of night was when the city really started hopping—or crawling or slithering. The nocturnal monsters came out for recreation, to make shopping trips, and just to go to work.

"We've all had a rough day, Beaux. We should take a break," Sheyenne said, putting her intangible hands on the very nice curve of her hips. "And I've got just the thing. A new game." She smiled, and I smiled back at her in an instinctive response.

I gave her my best interested leer. "Is it a private adult game, just between the two of us?" Since I was a zombie and she was a ghost, our romantic life posed certain challenges, but we knew how to make the best of things.

Giggling, Sheyenne shook her head. "No, it's a high-end board game that was released before the Big Uneasy."

"Back when people had time to play games," I said wistfully. "I was pretty good at Go Fish, and I know McGoo was learning how to play checkers, but the strategy keeps eluding him."

"Speaking of Officer McGoohan," Sheyenne said, "I called him, and he's coming over. Our game night is set, whether or not you want to play."

I looked down at the folders on my desk. "The cases don't solve themselves, but I'm not doing a very good job at it right now. Maybe some downtime will help."

I was feeling discouraged because I'd disappointed a client today. An ogre with a big heart and a gentle soul had lost his beloved pet lab rat named Mickey. I'd put up "Lost Rat" signs all over the Quarter and pursued many leads, until I discovered that Mickey had been taken to the animal shelter. I rushed there to retrieve him, but before I could arrive, a mad scientist had adopted all the rats and taken them back to his laboratory. Knowing it was a race against time, I tracked down the mad scientist ... and arrived moments too late. I did rescue Mickey, but only after the mad scientist had subjected his new pets to an oscillating electromagnetic experiment that dramatically increased the rats' brain capacities. By the time I reunited the slow-witted ogre with his beloved rat, Mickey had concocted a private scheme for world domination with his fellow super-intelligent rats, and Mickey wanted nothing more to do with his dull master. It was a real tragedy, and the ogre was brokenhearted.

Robin also had a big disappointment that day, losing a custody battle for a scarab demon who wanted to have her larvae back. The creature longed to nurture them, to hold onto them for as long as she could, but the grubs were bad seeds, hooligans causing all kinds of trouble in the Quarter by burrowing where they weren't wanted, ruining perfectly nice public parks. The mother beetle desperately wanted them back home, where she could care for them. Robin had made a passionate case, but the judge ruled to emancipate the grubs, since they were so close to pupating.

There wasn't much rejoicing in the Chambeaux & Deyer offices this evening. Why not play a game?

As Sheyenne set up the game in the conference room, I made myself another cup of truly awful coffee, then glanced in the mirror to flick a piece of lint from the round bullet hole in the center of my forehead. I assessed my features, which were handsome enough and well preserved. I decided I could forego a trip to the embalming parlor for a week or so.

McGoo came in the door still wearing his blue patrolman's uniform. "All right, what's the emergency?" He looked around and saw me, then broke into a stupid grin. "Hey Shamble, what do you call two zombies in a hot tub?"

I braced myself. "What?"

"Soup!" He laughed. The others didn't. We didn't want to encourage him.

Officer Toby McGoohan is a beat cop who had offended so many humans with his raw and politically insensitive humor that he got himself transferred to the Unnatural Quarter, where the monsters didn't like him much either, although they did tolerate him.

Sheyenne came out of the conference room, glowing. "It's better than an emergency, Officer McGoohan. It's game night."

Robin emerged to join us in the conference room, where Sheyenne proudly held out the box. "It's a zombie game called *Last Night on Earth*." She started taking out the cards and the pieces, the rule book. The package was well produced, and I stared at the ferocious photos of blood-thirsty zombies, their dead eyes, their gore-covered faces, naked teeth that could tear flesh.

"Is this supposed to be a spoof or something?" I asked.

McGoo picked up one of the cards that showed a particularly rotted and horrific shambling corpse. "Hey, this one reminds me of you, Shamble!"

"Still better than you look with a hangover," I said.

Heavy-hearted because of losing the larva custody case, Robin frowned at the box and the images. "This is rather insensitive to our zombie citizens. It perpetuates a stereotype."

"The game was made before the Big Uneasy," Sheyenne reminded her. "Back when the walking dead were seen as horrific cannibalistic monsters instead of upstanding members of the community."

I nodded. "Zombies who look and act like this in the Unnatural Quarter would be whisked off to a rehab and reconstruction facility. They need therapy."

"In this game, the zombies want brains," said Sheyenne, "and flesh and bodily fluids. It's dramatic. Come on, guys, get into the spirit of things."

We all agreed. Sheyenne set up the game using her poltergeist powers to lift the components and distribute them on the table, putting together several different boards to build a small town. While she worked, I asked, "How was your day, McGoo?"

"Awful as usual, but with a few good points." He reached into his pocket and pulled out a small delicate glass vial made filled with a swirling pearlescent lavender liquid. "I've got to take this into evidence."

"When did you start using perfume?" I asked.

"Not perfume. It's a magical substance. Very potent."

"Like a little blue pill?"

Sheyenne handed us a stack of character cards and set out little plastic figures for each one. "You need to choose who you're going to play as," she told us. "A human or a zombie."

"I choose zombie," I said.

McGoo picked human. He continued, "Remember that illicit poker house I busted six months ago? The back-alley den run by a genie?"

"Sure. The little imp gave a bad name to illegal gambling."

"We caught him using magically enhanced playing cards so that the house always won. He got sentenced to solitary confinement in his lamp, but today he was up for a parole hearing, and he requested that I speak on his behalf."

"As a character reference?" I asked. "That wasn't very smart. You put him away."

"I didn't have very nice things to say about him, so I was suspicious. Imagine my surprise when he secretly tried to bribe me with this." He held up the perfume bottle. "It's called Wish Stuff, a secret weapon that genies offer their clients. He said I could have whatever I most desired if I help him get out on probation."

"I'm not sure that's legal," Robin said. "What would you wish for, Officer McGoohan?"

I suggested, "He might wish to be more handsome."

"Wishes always backfire, Shamble. Instead, I reported him to the parole board, used this sample as evidence, and they denied his request and sentenced him to five more years of lockup inside his lamp. I'm supposed to deliver this to the evidence room at the station. But you said there was an emergency."

"Emergency game night," I said. "You can deliver it after we finish playing."

Sheyenne was anxious to get started. "This *Last Night on Earth* scenario takes place in the town of Woodinvale, population about fifteen hundred. There's a zombie outbreak."

"Isn't there always?" I asked.

"In Woodinvale, a zombie outbreak happens every thirty years or so. It's a recurring nightmare. And these are hungry zombies that like to chew on people. Our characters need to search through Woodinvale for townsfolk and save as many of them as possible from being eaten."

Robin was skeptical. "I still think it's fearmongering against zombies, and we shouldn't encourage that."

"It was from a simpler, innocent time," I said. "As the resident zombie here, let's just say I won't take offense."

Sheyenne started the game. She, Robin, and McGoo were the humans, and set out to explore Woodinvale in search of survivors. They split up almost immediately: why do people always do that? On my turn I got to move the zombies into position. They were slow, but there were a lot of them, and within a couple of turns I had McGoo pinned behind the counter in the town's small diner, desperately searching for anything he could use to defend himself. His character, Sheriff Anderson, finally found a weapon—a meat cleaver from the diner's kitchen—but I played a card that made it break, and the zombies overwhelmed him.

I cackled. "I really like this game, Sheyenne."

McGoo pulled out a new character, since his old one was now shambling across the board as a part of my zombie horde.

"Who are you this time, McGoo?"

He set his new plastic figure on the board. "Amanda, the prom queen. One of her special abilities is called 'Beautiful.'" He batted his eyes. I opened my mouth to say something but decided against it.

We were getting wrapped up in the game, watching the characters die—usually horribly, chewed up by hordes of undead with a bad case of the munchies. The besieged characters in Woodinvale seemed real to us: Doc Brody, Sherriff Anderson and his son Bobbie, Jennie Sty and her father, the drifter Jake Cartwright, even McGoo's prom queen.

"It's certainly an interesting alternate history," said Robin, at last getting distracted from her disappointing day.

"I'll bet some people even wish the Big Uneasy had never happened," McGoo said. "Although I'm not sure this apocalypse version is an improved scenario." He picked up the dice and rolled for combat, engrossed in the game, but my zombies rolled better. He added another wound token to his prom queen and realized that his character had just succumbed to the slavering horde—again. "*Awww*, shoot!" He pounded his fist on the table in frustration.

We have a sturdy conference room table, but McGoo's frustrated fist was even stronger. His blow jarred the surface, toppled some of the playing pieces. Worse, he knocked the delicate glass vial of Wish Stuff off the edge of the table, and it shattered on the floor.

He looked down at the spilling liquid and scowled. "*Awww*, shoot!" he said again. "That was evidence." McGoo scrambled to scoop up the pieces in his hands. The liquid ran over the shards of glass as he stuffed them in his shirt pocket, hoping to salvage something of the remains.

Extravagant lavender fumes curled up from the spilled liquid on the floor, like a fog bank erupting from the purple pool. We all began to cough. The mist filled the conference room.

"That doesn't smell like perfume, McGoo!" I waved my hands in front of me, but I couldn't see. The lavender mist seemed entirely unnatural, but the color quickly faded to a more common grayish-white fog, the kind often mischaracterized as pea soup, which is an entirely different color.

"Now what?" I asked.

Beside me, Sheyenne's ectoplasmic glow did little to illuminate the night. Robin and McGoo were also standing next to me, and as the fog cleared we found ourselves outside in a strange environment. We were on a paved county road with tall, dark evergreens looming around us. A full moon rode overhead.

In front of us I saw a sign that said

Welcome To Woodinvale
pop. 1500

A big, wet, red splatter of blood covered one side of the sign.

Not far away down the road, we heard a loud blood-curdling scream.

Considering the town sign and the eerie setting, I had a good guess what the horrific scream might mean.

McGoo didn't. "Do you think someone else had a bad dice roll?"

The scream rang out again, a woman's scream, but it sounded more furious than terrified. Even so, when someone screams it's natural either to run in terror or run to help. Good thing we were all in the latter category.

We didn't stop to consider how we'd been magically transported inside the game, or maybe this was just an advanced and ultra-realistic level of *Last Night on Earth*. We ran down the mist-slick highway overshadowed by pines, turned a sharp curve, and came upon a horrific frenzy of rotting flesh, blood, putrefaction, and cannibalism—in that order, although the cannibalism was still in its early stages and the victim in question was doing her very best not to become a victim.

She was an athletic young blonde dressed in jeans and a farm work shirt backed up against a battered old Ford pickup truck that was pulled off to the side of the road.

Her face and shirt were spattered with gore, and she wielded a big axe against a crowd of moaning zombies trying to rip the tender flesh from her bones.

These zombies didn't look like the nice ones you might meet in the Unnatural Quarter. Four of the shamblers already lay dead ... well, deader than they had been before meeting the girl with the axe. Severed body parts twitched and flopped on the pavement. She had been busy.

"Eat dirt, zombie!" She screamed and snarled, then swung the axe again with all her might, her lips drawn back in a grimace. "Take that for eating my thoroughbred horse!" Another blow of the axe knocked a head clean off of one of the slavering undead, and with a cool backstroke, barely even shifting her weight, she brought the weapon up into the crotch of another moaning zombie, which made him moan much more loudly. "And that's for my dog!"

Stumbling zombies collided with her pickup, arms outstretched, fingers hooked into claws. They closed in, oblivious to the whirling weapon. The sharpened steel head made wet hollow sounds as it impacted the bones, chopped shoulders, split ribcages down the middle. "And that's for my dad! You ate him right in the barn!"

Vengeance and adrenaline work well together, but the zombies kept coming, suffering from relentless munchies. Showing no common sense, Robin ran forward shouting, "Stop that! Leave her alone."

McGoo and I each drew our pistols. My .38 was fully loaded, and he had his police special revolver along with his police extra special revolver loaded with silver bullets. "Could we lend a hand, Miss?"

The young woman swung the axe again, but missed, which threw her off balance and gave the zombies a chance to lurch in. Two grabbed at her arm, tore her flannel shirt.

It was time to open fire. Given my preference, I'd rather not kill zombies—some of my best friends are zombies— but these weren't at all sociable. The creep who had torn the poor girl's shirt leered toward her with his mouth gaping to show his rotting teeth ready to clamp down on her arm. My first shot splattered his head. Brains and bits of skull spurted all over her face and the front of her shirt, but she didn't have time to show distaste because a second zombie was pressing her back against the truck, ready to rip out her throat. McGoo shot the second zombie.

The rest of the horde didn't mind. If they were starving for human flesh, that just meant a bigger portion for each of them.

Then the situation got worse, because the zombies realized that Robin and McGoo also smelled very tasty. Several shamblers turned and began lurching toward my two human friends, and McGoo had his hands full just defending Robin, while she looked around for a spare axe. He emptied his police special, then started using the more valuable bullets in the other revolver. Sheyenne flitted in, trying to distract the zombies, but her intangible form swooped right through their undead bodies, and they weren't impressed. The zombies kept coming.

The girl at the pickup truck shoved the bloody, rotting

corpses away, panted to catch her breath, then charged in beside me to help kill more of the horde. We exhibited good teamworking skills, and soon the undead lay in a more permanent state of death, strewn around us on the isolated highway.

The girl looked at us, exhausted and terrified. She was spattered with oozing blood and brains.

"Glad we could help," I said.

She turned to thank me, but when she realized I was a zombie too, she recoiled, ready to use the axe again. I held up my hands and backed away. "It's all right. I'm not with them."

"They're everywhere!" she said. "They rose from the grave and now they're wiping out the entire town." She hitched a deep breath, sobbing. "They attacked our farm. I tried to help defend it, but they killed my pa, my dog, my horse. I barely got out alive."

"What's your name?" Robin asked. Sheyenne drifted close, trying to reassure her, but the presence of a ghost wasn't as reassuring as Sheyenne had hoped.

"I'm Jenny Sty," she said, "from the Sty Farm down the road. I was heading into town to find Sheriff Anderson. He's got to know what's happening."

I remembered Jenny Sty from one of the character cards in the game. Even with the goop splashed all over her, she was prettier in person.

"I played Sheriff Anderson once," McGoo said. "It didn't turn out well."

"We don't quite know why we're here or how it happened," Robin said. "We were playing a game and …"

Jenny sobbed. "This isn't a game!" She looked at us again. "Why were you out here? Where's your car? Were you just walking alone down the highway? It's not safe."

I was concerned for Robin and McGoo, who were the most appetizing among us. I wanted to get them to safety. "Can you give us a ride into town?"

"Sure, if you help me fight any zombies that try to stop us."

"It's a deal," I said.

"Sheyenne and I will ride in back. Robin and McGoo, you join her up front. You're the most vulnerable."

"Who are you calling vulnerable?" McGoo asked.

"Who's the most likely zombie tasty treat?"

McGoo said decisively, "Shamble's right. You're up front with me, Robin."

Despite my stiff limbs, I managed to climb into the pickup bed. Under other circumstances, it might have been an enjoyable ride with my ghost girlfriend. It reminded me of happier times when we weren't in a real zombie apocalypse. And these were not cuddly zombies.

Jenny Sty drove along at top speed with her unmuffflered pickup roaring. Sitting in the back of the truck with the wind whipping around us, I spotted more zombies stumbling along the side of the road, lurching out of the trees. As we approached to the lights of Woodinvale, five zombies had wandered across the road like chickens in search of the other side.

Jenny mowed them down without even stopping. As the truck rolled over the bodies, Sheyenne and I jounced in the back of the pickup.

Ahead, oddly incongruous, we saw a rugged man standing by the side of the road. He looked well worn, as if he'd been washed on the heavy-duty cycle and left to drip dry. He extended his thumb in classic hitchhiker pose. Jenny slammed on the brakes, slewed the truck to a stop. McGoo stuck his head out the passenger window. "Not a good night for a walk, Mister. Too many zombie pedestrians."

"Can you give me a lift to town?" he asked. "I'm Jake— Jake Cartwright."

"Hitchhiking is dangerous," Sheyenne said.

"There's room here in the back," I said, and helped him climb into the bed.

Even before the drifter managed to settle down, Jenny roared off again toward the outskirts of town. More groups of zombies lurched along in the ditches, but the pickup was going too fast for them to attack.

"If Woodinvale has a population of only 1500, where are they getting all these reanimated bodies?" I wondered.

Sheyenne said, "Maybe they have a special storage area somewhere."

The drifter had a grim expression as he peered ahead down the road. The town lights looked warm and comforting, but they also served as bug lights attracting bloodthirsty zombies like moths on a summer night.

Before we reached the main buildings of Woodinvale, we rolled past a brightly lit diner with several cars parked in front, including a sheriff's police cruiser. Jenny hit the brakes again, hard, spitting gravel under the tires, and she swerved into the diner's parking lot. I held on hard, preferring not to be thrown headfirst over the cab. An instant after the pickup ground to a halt, the driver's door popped open and Jenny scrambled out. McGoo and Robin emerged from the other side.

"Sheriff!" Jenny yelled as she ran toward the diner. We followed.

"I could use a bite to eat," said Jake the hitchhiker.

The diner was crowded with frightened townspeople, and frightened people were apparently as hungry as zombies on the prowl. Every customer had a plate of food piled in front of them. The cook was working overtime in the back.

"Sheriff, there's zombies out there!" Jenny said.

Sheriff Anderson was standing at the counter facing all the people who had gathered for shelter. "We know, Jenny. I'm rallying the citizens. We've got to defend ourselves. This is my town and I'm taking it back."

The angry and terrified people in the diner had armed themselves with baseball bats, sledge hammers, axes, hunting rifles. One man even held a mop.

"They're back again," said a weary-looking older man. I recognized him from the townsfolk card: Doc Brody. "It's happening all over. Some of us remember the last outbreak thirty years ago." He glanced at Sheriff Anderson. "We thought we took care of it back then."

"Not good enough, obviously," said the sheriff. "This time we've got to wipe them out. Completely."

Jake walked up to the counter just as the diner cook, a hard-muscled man who looked like a drill sergeant emerged with two more plates of eggs and hash browns. "Sam, can I get a cup of coffee?"

"I'll have one too," I said. "Best to stay awake. This is going to be a long night."

McGoo ordered breakfast with extra bacon. "Game universe calories don't count," he said. "We're stuck here until we can figure out how to get back to our normal world of resurrected monsters and mythical creatures."

"A world that makes sense," I said.

Sherriff Anderson continued to address the townspeople. "Zombies have come back to Woodinvale, but they can be killed—again. Beware, if they bite you, you'll be infected. You become one of them." His voice hitched. "My own son Bobby …"

"Oh, Sheriff," Robin said with deep sympathy. Apparently, she hadn't read through the entire rulebook.

Doc Brody said, "Thank God the outbreak is localized to Woodinvale. If this spreads across the country, it might mean the end of the human race." He looked solemnly at all the people clustered in the diner. "This could be our last night on Earth."

"Good title," I said.

As Sam the diner cook brought our coffee and served McGoo his plate of eggs, bacon, hash browns and a side of pancakes, I leaned closer. "You know this is all because of that Wish Stuff you took from the genie."

McGoo fell to his eggs, mashing them into his hash browns. "The stuff must be defective, because I never wished to get into this game."

"Maybe it's a generic brand of wish stuff with unknown side effects."

He patted his front pocket where the broken shards of the bottle remained. "It won't do us any good, and now my shirt is soaked with the goop."

I scanned the people in the diner, recognizing many of them from the character cards. I recalled that some had died horribly in our game—Sheriff Anderson had been torn apart in this very diner—but now they were back. Was it all different now? Since Sheyenne, McGoo, Robin, and I had entered the game itself, would that change the outcome? We couldn't know, and I didn't want to stick around to find out.

"We've got to get out of here, McGoo. Can't you undo what you did?"

He munched on a strip of bacon. "Why are you blaming me?"

"Because you're usually the one that messes things up."

"You've got me there." He concentrated on his eggs and hash browns again.

The diner cook came back around, holding a cup of coffee for himself. "Is the food all right?"

"Delicious," McGoo said with his mouth full. "I need to keep up my strength if we're going to be fighting zombies."

"He usually just solves cases with zombies," I said.

"I wouldn't call attention to that bullet hole in your head," said Sam the cook. "Zombies don't have a good reputation around here right now."

"I'm a different sort of zombie," I said.

"They're back and they'll keep coming back," groaned Doc Brody.

"Here they come!" shouted a young man in a high school letterman's jacket. He pressed his hands and face against the window of the diner. "Must be a hundred of them."

Sheriff Anderson unholstered his revolver, while McGoo hurriedly finished his breakfast. The Woodinvale townspeople gathered their makeshift weapons, ready to make a last stand. The man with the mop held the wooden handle and looked ferocious.

I stood next to McGoo and told Robin to come closer. Sheyenne hovered in front of us. "We'll do our best to protect you two," I said. "You're my friends, and I don't want you munched."

"We don't want to be munched either," said McGoo, scraping the last of his eggs with a stray pancake. "If I had another vial of that Wish Stuff … but all I've got is a sticky mess." He dabbed his fingertips to the stain on his pocket.

The first zombie smashed through the diner's plate-glass window. The townspeople screamed. Rotting hands stretched through the broken glass, grabbing the kid in the letterman jacket who didn't move fast enough. Another window shattered and five more of the undead pressed in, their faces ragged, greenish, and rotting.

Since it was game night, I hadn't brought along extra bullets and I rapidly emptied my .38. Sheriff Anderson shot his revolver until he had nothing left but empty clicks. The townspeople with rifles opened fire.

And the zombies kept coming.

The man with the mop charged into the fray as walking dead pushed through the smashed window. More polite zombies actually entered through the diner's main door.

"This isn't a fun game anymore," I said to Sheyenne. "Too realistic."

She looked forlorn. "It was fun when it was just a game."

"We had a bad day to start with," Robin said.

The hitchhiker gulped his coffee and stood, cracked his knuckles, and joined Sheriff Anderson. "Ready to do this again, Sherriff?"

"There's always trouble when you show up," said the sheriff.

Since my pistol was out of bullets, I just tried to look threatening, hoping that might protect Robin and McGoo. Dozens of zombies lurched their way through the jagged glass, which did little to help their physical integrity. I preferred the more friendly zombies in the Quarter.

Though I could tell Robin was frightened, she didn't say anything. She picked up one of the silver napkin containers in one hand and a salt shaker in the other, ready to defend herself. She had faced plenty of difficult court cases, and sometimes she lost, like today in the larva-custody battle. But this was serious. I could see in her face that she genuinely expected to die.

McGoo was also pale and sick. He didn't even have a stupid joke for the occasion. I didn't know what I'd do if anything happened to them.

"But it's just a game!" Sheyenne insisted.

"It's a very realistic and engaging game," I said. "And now we're screwed."

Maybe it really would be our last night on Earth.

The zombies crashed inside, flooding the diner as if this were the lunch rush and Sam had offered free beer with every meal. I saw people fall. Jenny swung her axe again and again, and then the zombies were upon her. Other victims fell screaming, their skin torn, their bodies opened up as the zombies feasted.

"McGoo, you've got to make a wish," I said desperately as we backed against the poorly defended counter. "You didn't use all of the stuff. Smear the stain on your fingers. Maybe there's enough magic left in the residue."

McGoo dabbed at the sticky substance that had leaked out of the broken bottle and into his shirt. "But there's not much."

"Then wish really, really hard."

As the zombies lurched closer, McGoo pawed at his shirt, got his fingers as wet as possible, and started chanting over and over, squeezing his eyes shut. "There's no place like home! There's no place like home!"

The rest of the trapped diner patrons were falling under the zombie onslaught, and their deaths were horrifying, but they were all nonplayer characters—and we were *real.*

McGoo pressed his palm harder against his wet shirt and pushed his eyes shut, grimacing like a man who had been constipated for four days. "There's no place like home! I wish I was back in the Unnatural Quarter!"

The zombies lunged toward us, groping hands outstretched—

And then they were just pictures on the cards.

We were back in the Chambeaux & Deyer conference room. The din of moaning zombies crunching bone and slurping flesh, the horrified screaming and gunfire, suddenly changed to deafening silence. We stood shaken, staring at one another, and then we simultaneously began to laugh with an edge of hysteria.

"That was close!" McGoo held up his sticky hands. "Man, I wish—"

I immediately clamped a hand over his mouth. "Let's not take any chances, McGoo. Go change your shirt and wash your hands."

He realized what he'd almost said. "You're right, Shamble." He began unbuttoning his blue uniform blouse.

Sheyenne looked down at the scattered pieces and cards of *Last Night on Earth* and silently began to put the game away. "That's enough for tonight. No point in doing another round."

Robin nodded, still shaken. "I … I should get back to working on my cases. That's what I do for fun."

"Sorry game night didn't turn out the way you wanted, Sheyenne," I said. "Thanks for wanting to bring us all together."

She closed the box for *Last Night on Earth*. "We better store this in a safe place and not risk playing it again." Even her ectoplasmic form looked wrung out. "Next time, we could try something different, something safer."

"What did you have in mind?" I asked, still hoping for one of the private adult games.

"The same company has a weird western game that looks fun. It's called *Shadows of Brimstone*, and I think—"

"Not now, Spooky," I said. "Not now."

Cold Dead Turkey

When an Aztec mummy stopped me on the streets of the Unnatural Quarter, I knew it had to be an important problem. "Excuse me, are you Dan Shamble? Zombie P.I.?"

"*Chambeaux,*" I corrected automatically, because so many people—both naturals and unnaturals—make the mistake. "But yes, that's me—of Chambeaux & Deyer Investigations."

The day was bright and sunny, and we had paused under a street light where two precariously balanced werewolves were stringing holiday lights. One mockingly dangled a fistful of mistletoe over the other, demanding a kiss. The second werewolf said, "Not with your ugly furry muzzle!"

Across the street, a skeleton lounged with a saxophone against another lamppost, ready to play a mournful holiday tune, but it was all for show because the skeleton wasn't a very effective sax player, due to his lack of lungs. Skeleton musicians usually stick to playing the piano.

The Aztec mummy was withered and shriveled. The remnants of his raisin-like eyes were set deeply into hollows in his face. He hobbled along, his back bent, his knees of the extra-knobby variety. His clothes were gaudy and colorful, the finest Aztec chic. He extended a gnarled hand, and I shook it, careful not to break any bones. Mummies can be so brittle, and most refuse to be rehydrated as a matter of pride.

"How can I help you, Mr.—?"

The mummy cleared his throat, and a small moth fluttered out. "Kashewpetl." I realized it was his Aztec name rather than a head cold. "And I need you to track down my turkey. A special *wish turkey*." He leaned forward, and his intent raisin eyes transfixed me. "I need to have it by Christmas."

"That's the day after tomorrow," I said.

"I know! We better hurry."

We walked past an auto repair shop where two vampires were placing a large inflatable snowman in front of a sign that said: "Special Holiday Blowout Tire Sale!"

"I'm happy to hear your case, Mr. Kashewpetl." It would certainly be better than my early morning duties.

I had just finished delivering a little holiday cheer—serving divorce papers to a recently separated reptile-demon couple. Due to financial circumstances, they were forced to cohabitate their single-family lair apartment, and the male reptile demon had hired Chambeaux & Deyer to take care of the paperwork. Robin had filed the correct forms, and I had to present the papers to the soon-to-be-ex-wife-demon. A formality, but it wasn't one of my happiest duties.

The female reptile demon answered the door and took one look at my gray skin, my Fedora tilted down so that it mostly covered the bullet hole in my forehead. I tried to smile, but she curled back scaly lips to expose needle-like teeth. "What do you want? We're not buying." Her forked tongue flicked in and out.

"I assure you there's absolutely no charge," I said. "Mrs. Algotha? Frieda Algotha?"

A big, lumbering, scaly male demon lurked in the hall. "Who is it?"

"Some zombie selling subscriptions."

"Not selling." I handed her the paperwork. "Just serving."

That was when she really went into a hissy fit, snapping and snarling, and her husband—our client—snarled just as loudly back at her. Their scaly tails lashed, smashing into the wall, cracking the plaster, knocking down knickknacks. Then the demons began blaming each other, and Frieda Algotha stormed off to lock herself in a room. "My mother always told me I should have married Bill!"

I stood there awkwardly, wanting very much to be in some different kind of hell. The big, ferocious crocodile guy sulked in the foyer. "I had to do it, Mr. Chambeaux," he said, as if I were his bartender. He wore a big frown on jaws that looked powerful enough to snap a Volkswagen in two. "Christmas is always rough on cold-blooded creatures. This one's going to be worse than usual." He closed the door on me.

Give me a good murder (or re-murder) case, a missing creatures problem, a stolen items recovery any day. I hated divorce cases. I hoped the Aztec mummy had something a lot more interesting for me....

"Would you like to meet me back at our offices? I can set up an appointment." Sheyenne, my beautiful ghost girlfriend, is our office manager and organizes all of our paperwork. My human lawyer partner, Robin Deyer, has a caseload as large as mine.

When all the bizarre supernatural creatures returned to the world more than a decade ago during the unexpected cosmic event of the Big Uneasy, there had been quite an uproar until all the monsters settled into a semblance of normal life in the Unnatural Quarter. Everybody—naturals and unnaturals—just wanted to get through the days, and nights, as best they could, and even the unnaturals experienced as many everyday problems as regular people did. From our main offices, Robin took care of their legal needs, and I was handy whenever somebody needed a detective. A zombie detective.

"I would rather talk to you right now," the mummy rasped. "Time is of the essence." He indicated a sign in a clothing shop with giant painted letters touting: "Christmas Countdown! The End of the Sale Is Near!" He set off. "Let's walk."

Because his back was hunched, and his legs so bent, he moved with an exaggerated oscillating gait. "Are you sure?" I nodded to his stiff joints.

"It's just the way I was made. Aztec mummies are bound up and preserved in a sitting position. Unlike those uppity Egyptian mummies, we're *naturally* dried, not wrapped up in linens, and we're buried in a cloth sack instead of stuffy sarcophagi and fancy tombs. Who needs a pyramid, anyway? And nobody scooped *my* brain out through my nose. It's still perfectly intact, thank you."

I could see I had struck a nerve, so I changed the subject. "Tell me about your turkey."

We passed a group of banshee Christmas carolers who sang their hearts out, and all the nearby plate glass windows trembled in fear.

"Right, let me explain. I needed the wish turkey to get my favorite sled back," said Kashewpetl, an explanation that did not serve the purpose of explaining anything.

"Your favorite missing sled?" I asked.

"My precious toy from when I was a boy. Ah, the good times I had, the perfect sled, constructed with the best jungle materials—the finest sled in the whole Yucatan! My cousins and I would climb the slopes of Popocatepetl, one of the largest volcanoes in Central America—seventeen thousand feet high! Great powder on the snow slopes, at least when Popocatepetl wasn't erupting lava."

The mummy let out a desiccated sigh. "Those were the best days of my life, innocent times, perfect days when my parents and I would go see the ritual temple sacrifice, when we kids would run through the jungle and play Dodge the Jaguar ... when I had my first love—a girlfriend so special that I still remember her even a thousand years later."

Another long sigh. This time, two moths came out of his lungs. "Sweet, beautiful Suzitoq. We used to sled together. I'd put her in front of me, and we'd slide down the treacherous ice slopes. When we got to the bottom, I would steal a kiss. Good times!" Then he grew much more somber. "Then she went sledding with one of my rivals, Burtputl, but he used a far inferior sled and it broke. Suzitoq tumbled over a cliff." He hung his shriveled head. "I never forgave Burtputl."

We passed a small stand where a saggy-faced ghoul was selling gray-brown snow cones. I asked the mummy if he wanted one—he was my client, after all—but he shook his head and continued his story.

"Suzitoq is long dead now, but I kept that sled for the rest of my life as a reminder of those golden days. I never married, became a bitter old man—I admit it. I saved enough money so that I could be thoroughly mummified. But after I died, Burtputl stole my sled, and it's been lost all these centuries. He probably wrecked it." Kashewpetl snorted. "I'd do anything to have it back. That's why I need your help, Mr. Chambeaux."

"What does that have to do with a missing turkey?"

"Not just any turkey," said Kashewpetl. "A *wish* turkey."

That must be a key part to the case. "So what's a wish turkey?"

"A special turkey that I raised from a chick. The Chosen One. I tattooed arcane symbols on its hide, tied special amulets to its feet to infuse the bird with the most potent Aztec magic. I pampered it, fattened it, even brought beautiful lady turkeys to his cage. It was necessary to give my wish turkey the most hedonistic lifestyle a turkey could want, considering what was to happen to him."

I bought one of the brown snow cones from the ghoul vendor. I would rather have had a beer at the Goblin Tavern after work—and I intended to do so anyway—but for now I sucked on the dirty ice of the cone. "And what was going to happen to him?"

"Ritual sacrifice," said Kashewpetl.

Of course.

"The holiday season holds a very special magic, a secret and fuzzy kind of Christmas magic. After I sacrificed my wish turkey, I could cook him up and extract the sacred wishbone. Then, if I cracked the wishbone, I could wish for *anything I wanted*." His shrunken raisin eyes blazed brighter. "I could have what I desired most in the whole world. I could wish for my sled back."

I wondered why he wouldn't simply wish for Suzitoq back, but I doubted the Aztec mummy had thought this through. So, I asked the more compelling question. "What on earth does an Aztec ritual sacrifice have to do with the magic of *Christmas*? The two aren't the least bit connected, on either a cultural or a religious basis."

Kashewpetl raised his arms so quickly I was afraid his elbow joints would snap. "One mustn't question! One mustn't doubt. One mustn't think too hard about it, or the magic fades away. And the magic of the wish turkey wishbone is powerful indeed. Don't diminish it, Mr. Chambeaux."

I slurped on my brown snow cone, spit out a bit of

gravel, and metaphorically zipped my lips shut. "It's none of my business, and not part of the case. So tell me what happened. Your turkey's gone missing?"

"Yes, he got out of his cage somehow. I never imagined he could figure it out—turkeys aren't the brightest animals in the menagerie, you know. But I need him back in the next day or two, when the magic is strongest. He's out there somewhere, probably lost and alone and hungry."

"Did your wish turkey suspect what you were going to do to it? Did he know he was about to be sacrificed?" It would have given it the motive to flee.

Kashewpetl gave me a strange look. "There are times when he can't even find his water dish right there in his own cage."

"I see. Well, if you come by the offices later on—" We stepped across the street to get to the other side—I wondered if that was what turkeys did too, and for the same reason. I wasn't watching, and suddenly a delivery truck barreled toward us. The truck driver honked his horn and swerved to avoid hitting us. I leaped to one side as I grabbed the mummy, since his hobbling gait was insufficient for leaping away from large careening vehicles.

The driver was a zombie wearing a trucker's cap and work overalls. "Watch where you're going, idiots!" He screeched to a halt, then leaned out the driver's side window, ready to yell something else, then his face changed. "Dan? Dan Chambeaux? Man, I'm sorry about that."

I recognized Steve Halsted, my "dirt buddy," a zombie who had risen from the grave the same night I did.

Recently, Steve had been running deliveries around the Quarter and he sometimes served as a long-haul trucker. "What's your hurry, Steve? Driving that fast, you're going to hit somebody who isn't already dead."

He looked flustered. "Sorry, I'm carrying a load of fresh ripe toadstools, and I've got to deliver them before the spores go bad. On my way!" He peeled off in the truck.

Kashewpetl said, "I'll head back home to keep searching. Here's where you can find me." He wrote his address on a scrap of torn bandage that looked as if it had been ripped from an old Egyptian mummy, maybe out of spite.

"I have to get back to the office, then I'll go file a police report," I said. "We'll find your turkey, Mr. Kashewpetl, and we'll find him before Christmas, I promise."

"Thanks. It just wouldn't be a holiday season without a ritual sacrifice."

Sitting at her desk in the Chambeaux & Deyer offices, Sheyenne was positively glowing when she saw me. Ghosts tend to do that. I gave her an air kiss, because that's all we could do—our lips passed right through, but I felt an ectoplasmic thrill regardless. Since I was a zombie, it had been a long time since my heart went pitter-pat, but at least Sheyenne made it go *thud* a little faster.

"Papers served on the Algothas," I said. "Not much Ho-Ho-Ho going on in that house today."

"Sorry, Beaux. Not everybody can have a perfect relationship like us."

"We don't exactly have a perfect relationship, Spooky, considering we can't even touch, or hold hands, or kiss, or do the stuff that happens after the ellipsis dots when the door closes at the end of an old romance novel."

"Being intangible does have its drawbacks," she admitted. She straightened the papers using her poltergeist power and stuffed them in a file. I told Sheyenne about Kashewpetl, and she filled out the paperwork for the intake of the new client, then scolded me for not discussing the appropriate fees. The mummy had looked so intense and distraught that I hadn't had the heart, but I understood it was necessary.

Without Sheyenne keeping us on the commercial straight-and-narrow, Robin would be a sucker for sob stories and do every case as pro bono. She's a bleeding-heart, which is why all the monsters in the Quarter come to her when they have a meaningful case. As a zombie, I was just as relentless as a detective, though a bit colder. Working together, we get the job done, solve the cases, and keep our customers satisfied.

"Robin's with a new client," Sheyenne said, "if you want to meet her."

We run a tight office and know each other's cases, even when my detective work and Robin's legal work don't overlap. I knocked politely before opening her office door; inside, she sat at her desk, facing the new client. Robin's a beautiful young African-American woman from an upper middle-class family. She went to college, got her law degree, but instead of choosing to work for some wealthy corporation, she wanted to help the downtrodden, and there were very few who were more downtrodden than the unnaturals after the turmoil of the Big Uneasy. Here in the Quarter, it seemed that something truly unusual came up every day.

Such as the client sitting across from her right now.

I had never seen a Medusa with flowers in her hair before. The gorgon sat in a chair wearing a hippie peasant dress covered with frilly appliques. She smelled of patchouli mixed with dry reptile. Her hair, which was a nest of serpents, swirled and writhed. I cringed, knowing that Medusas have a penchant for turning people to stone much like their unrelated but just as petrifying counter-parts, cockatrices and basilisks.

This Medusa, though, was an obvious peacenik, with a peace symbol pendant hanging down from her scabrous neck. Each one of the serpents was blindfolded with a little yellow ribbon tied around its head. The fanged mouths each bit down over a rosebud, neutralizing the fangs.

I smiled and stepped in. Did I mention that we see these sort of cases every day?

"Hello, Dan!" Robin sat forward in her chair, looking thoroughly un-petrified. On the desk sat a yellow legal pad and an animated pencil that was automatically scribbling notes. The pad and pencil set had been a gift last Christ-mas, when we'd helped the actual Santa Claus recover his stolen Naughty-and-Nice list. "Meet Saffron, my new client."

The gorgon turned to me, and all of the blindfolded and flower-filled snakes also swiveled in my direction, as if looking for a target. When Saffron smiled, she showed multiple fangs. "Pleased to meet you, Mr. Chambeaux."

I had taken off my Fedora and hung up my sport jacket, and I was ready to help. "Need any zombie detective work?"

"Ms. Saffron is seeking legal advice on some rather pressing but esoteric issues," Robin explained.

The Medusa sounded sweet and somewhat vapid. "What do you think, Mr. Chambeaux? Wouldn't you like world peace, an end to conflict and strife, no more hunger or disease, every single person living a happy life, no more prejudice?"

"I suppose that would be nice." I didn't think she was actually looking for an insightful answer. "Sounds like a pretty long Christmas list."

"All good citizens should wish for those things, and if we pull together, if every one of us helped the poor and the needy, if we just stopped hating one another, the world would be a better place."

"I can't argue with that. But, uh, was there a legal question involved?"

"That's what we're trying to determine," Robin said.

Saffron put her elbows on Robin's desk, and her snakes drifted around as if they were all stoned. "Now, I know that stealing is wrong, but what if you steal with the best of intentions?"

Robin frowned. "The law is the law. You can't just steal things."

"But what if a loved one was dying of a disease and some evil corporation was keeping the cure locked away?

Wouldn't I be justified in stealing it, not just for my loved one but for curing the world?"

"I doubt any jury would convict you," Robin said, "but it's still against the law to steal private property."

"And what if a large army had the actual secret to ending wars forever so that no one else has to die in combat, but they keep it locked up because war is big business? Wouldn't I be justified in stealing that secret, giving it to the world, and bringing peace?"

"Your justifications sound convincing," Robin repeated, "but you might still go to jail."

"You don't mess with big business or the military industrial complex," I warned.

When the Medusa sighed, all of her snakes went limp with disappointment. "At least I'd go to prison with a clean conscience." Saffron still wasn't ready to let the problem go, though. "But what if—"

I backed out of the office, knowing that she might ask the perennial question about dancing angels and pinheads. "This one's above my pay grade, but Robin can solve it if anyone can."

I was glad I only had to find a lost turkey.

At the UQPD precinct station, I met Officer Toby McGoohan adjusting his cap as he was leaving the station to go on his afternoon rounds. He stopped and saw me, and a grin broadened on his freckled face. "Hey, Shamble. Maybe you can help me with a question."

I knew I was in for trouble. "What, McGoo?"

"If the Zombie Apocalypse happens in Vegas, would it stay in Vegas?"

Yeah, I'd shambled right into that one. McGoo is my BHF, my Best Human Friend. Through bad life choices and just plain dogged persistence, we had both reached for big dreams and successful careers—and we both ended up here, just trying to get by. He'd been on the beat for years; we helped each other on cases; we had always hung out together when I was a living human detective, and we still hung out even after I'd been murdered. It took him awhile to get used to his undead pal, but friendships last longer than rigor mortis.

"Enough jokes, time to get down to business. I need your help, McGoo."

"You need a lot of help," he wisecracked. "Official business? Or something we can talk about over beers tonight?"

"Official police business. I need to file a missing turkey report."

McGoo took it in stride. As I said, unusual cases crop up in the Quarter every day. He led me back to his cubicle and rummaged in his desk drawer. "I think we have a form for that."

It turned out, to my surprise, that half a dozen missing turkeys had been reported in the last week, all across the Quarter. "Is that unusual?" I asked.

He shrugged. "It's the holiday season, and everyone wants a turkey dinner."

"But most grocery store chains have ridiculously cheap

sales on holiday turkeys. Why risk jail time instead of just buying one of the five-dollar specials?"

McGoo's eyes narrowed. "Don't try to talk logic when it comes to turkey thieves. They're the worst—take it from me."

McGoo had a small cluttered desk in the main pool, but he rarely spent any time there because he's the sort of cop who likes to be walking his beat, seeing problems with his own eyes—and picking up fodder for more bad jokes. He handed me the sheet. "You're perfectly capable of filling out a missing-turkey form on your own."

"Thanks for the vote of confidence," I said while he amused himself by playing a game of Cockroach Crush on his phone. Sadly, I couldn't actually finish the form. I knew some of the answers: name of owner, date the bird went missing. Under distinguishing marks I wrote down "Aztec ceremonial tattoos marked on hide, charm bangles tied onto feet." But as to the details of the night on which it had gone missing, or even what names the turkey responded to, I was at a loss. I would have to go back to the Aztec mummy to get the final details.

"Get started with this, McGoo." I slid the incomplete form over to him. "I'll come back with more information later today. I've got to see a mummy about a turkey."

Even from halfway down the suburban street it was plain which house belonged to Kashewpetl. It was a modest rambler, but the garage was a ziggurat, a stair-stepped pyramid with a small sacrificial altar on top where the mummy intended to sacrifice his wish turkey on Christmas Eve. Right now the platform had a bird feeder and a wind vane. The mailbox was adorned with Aztec symbols.

Kashewpetl's neighbor, though, was obviously an *Egyptian* mummy, his house built in the shape of a pyramid, the sides sloped to a perfect triangular apex, only two stories high. Considering the slope of the angled ceilings, I doubted that the upstairs or attic would have much usable space.

Not content with pink lawn flamingoes, the Egyptian mummy neighbor had a sphinx in the front yard (though only a small decorative model) and a statue of Anubis. I saw the Egyptian mummy out in the yard holding a garden hose, watering a hedge between his and the Aztec mummy's property.

Being neighborly as he saw me shamble along, he raised a bandaged hand, but when I turned toward the Aztec mummy's door, he looked away in a huff. There seemed to be no love lost between the neighbors.

I knocked on Kashewpetl's door and entered. The Aztec mummy had been sitting in a recliner chair that perfectly accommodated his bent-over posture. "I need a few more details for the missing turkey report, and I'd also like to have a look at the cage, see if we can figure out how it got loose."

Kashewpetl used the remote to switch off the TV. He was obviously a single man who lived alone, someone who dwelled in the past—more than a thousand years of it. On the wall hung the large ornate disk of an Aztec calendar with the words "Today's Date Is ..." The calendar was one of the extended post-2012 holocaust editions with extra dates added. A sticky note marked with festive holly leaves and berries marked *Christmas Day!!!* only two days hence.

Kashewpetl shuffled to the back room. "I gave the turkey his very own bedroom—the master bedroom in fact, nicer than mine."

In the hallway hung two framed pictures, one of an Egyptian pyramid and the other showing a bandaged mummy—both obscured by the circle/slash of the universal No symbol. I frowned at the anti-Egyptian sentiment. "I take it you're not on the best of terms with the pyramid next door?"

The Aztec mummy's face was too desiccated to feature a genuine frown. "We don't see eye socket to eye socket— mainly because he's full of himself and still living in another age. He's uppity, gets his bandages cleaned at a high-priced rewrapping and styling salon, then makes insulting comments that Aztec mummies aren't real mummies, that we're just pretenders, naturally desiccated, with no embalming process." He looked at me. "That's enough reason to hate your neighbor, isn't it?"

"I suppose so," I said. I take a lot of pride in that, keeping my body in shape—which includes regular touch-ups at the embalming parlor—so I don't rot and fall apart like too many of my less-conscientious zombie comrades.

"And his girlfriend is even worse, a total dingbat," Kashewpetl continued. "His name is Eff-Tup. I did some digging in the city records, found out that he wasn't even nobility back in Egypt! That he went through the whole expensive mummification process due to a paperwork error. Eff-Tup was just a traveling papyrus salesman, and now he thinks he owns the Nile." He snorted, making a hollow whistle through his empty nasal cavities. "Once I get my wish turkey back and I have my favorite sled, I'm not going to let him use it. Ever."

I didn't think there were many toboggan hills in the Quarter, but I let the mummy have his dreams.

Inside the turkey's master bedroom, the walls had been strung with Christmas decorations, tinsel, glittering ornaments, a small set of speakers with an MP3 player and Christmas carols playing on a constant loop.

"What are all the festive decorations for?" I asked.

"To celebrate the season, let him feel the holiday cheer. I figured if the turkey was marked for death, I should at least keep him happy. After all, he's granting me my wish to get my favorite present back."

"Do you think the wish turkey felt that he was fulfilling a destiny? That he had a well accomplished life?"

The Aztec mummy's stiff neck tilted forward at an odd angle. "Mr. Chambeaux, no matter what the circumstances, there's really not much more that a standard turkey can hope for."

The cage had a simple hook-and-eye latch that had been popped open to leave the door wide. Inside was a water dish, a food dish, and an expansive bed stuffed with goose down (*Would that bother a turkey?* I wondered.); a postage-stamp-sized picture of Kashewpetl hung on the cage wall. Gold chains and colorful ribbons dangled from the bars for decoration, and a plum-sized, mirrored disco ball hung from the roof. Decadent and hedonistic indeed, if you were a turkey.

I looked at the simple hook and eye, flipping it back and forth with my clumsy fingers. A turkey could easily have knocked it loose. "Are you certain he didn't get out by himself?"

Kashewpetl rolled his tiny shriveled eyes. "Turkeys can drown in a rainstorm because they aren't smart enough to close their beaks when they look up into the pouring rain."

"Just checking all the bases." I raised the other obvious possibility. "Do you think someone stole it?"

"Kidnapped my turkey? Why would anyone do that?"

Sometimes the client doesn't see what's right in front of him. "You said it's a *wish* turkey. Maybe somebody else wanted the wishbone."

He looked horrified. "Oh no! Mr. Chambeaux, we've got to find my turkey before Christmas! If we don't, everyone's holiday will be ruined."

Not the turkey's, I thought.

Back at the Chambeaux & Deyer offices, late at night before midnight on Christmas Eve, Robin worked through dinner on the convoluted new legal case of the Medusa with a conscience. I needed to call McGoo (for the fifth time) to find out if he had any leads on my lost turkey—or on any of the lost turkeys, because what happened to one gobbler might have happened to another.

We gathered in the conference room to discuss the day's work, partly to exchange information and leads, partly as a support group. "My new client is an Aztec mummy," I said. "He's lost some kind of magical turkey that he thinks will be able to restore a long-lost sled he had as a child. He wants to give it to himself as a Christmas present."

"A sled?" Sheyenne asked. "Can't he just buy a new one? For a lot less than what he'd be paying in our fees."

"Nostalgia," I said, as if that explained everything. "That's reason enough for Kashewpetl."

Robin said, "Bless you."

"So, did you resolve the moral dilemma with the hippie gorgon?" I asked.

Robin sighed. "Saffron has a deep abiding sense of right and wrong, but she has no clue about the law. She thinks that if she steals something for altruistic reasons, then it's not stealing. I tried to explain, but she keeps wanting me to find a loophole."

"Did she tell you what she stole?" Sheyenne asked.

"Some kind of magical talisman that makes wishes come true," Robin was obviously skeptical. "Chalk it up to fairy dust and the like. I believe Saffron is the type to plan her grocery shopping trips according to her horoscope."

"Hmm, a talisman that makes wishes come true? Sounds like my client's missing wish turkey."

"A wish turkey, did you say?" Robin looked at me. "She did mention something about a wishbone. She and her boyfriend acquired it, but I think he's just doing it to keep her happy. He's an Egyptian mummy named Eff-Tup."

I sat up straight. I couldn't believe the solution was right there. "They took that wish turkey out of the cage in Kashewpetl's house, right next door. We should make a pyramid call to Eff-Tup and Saffron, so I can retrieve my client's stolen property!"

Robin looked horrified. "But you can't use the information from *my client* against them! It's a conflict of interest for me. Not ethical."

"But we're doing it for the right reasons," I said. "Saffron would certainly understand that." Suddenly it all became clear to me: The Medusa wanted world peace, an end to war, the cures for all sickness, an end to poverty. That was how she intended to use the wish turkey. Kashewpetl just wanted an old sled back, a trivial and selfish wish. There shouldn't be any contest as to which one had the better *reason* for sacrificing the magical turkey.

But from our experience in dealing with Satanic contracts and practical jokester genies, wishes had a way of coming true—but in unexpected and often disastrous ways. I realized to my horror that one way to end all poverty, sickness, and war, and to bring about world peace, would be to simply wipe out all life on Earth.

Not exactly a solution I would like to have. I wondered how powerful that wish turkey really was, and I decided that wasn't a risk I wanted to take.

"It's not a conflict of interest," I said to Robin. "Stealing is stealing, whether or not Saffron's wish sounds better than my client's.

Robin hung her head. "You're right, Dan. And the law is the law. We'd better bring in the police, though. We'll get the turkey back, hold it in custodial care, then let the courts decide."

"That'll take until well past Christmas," Sheyenne said.

"There's always next Christmas," I suggested. I called McGoo, so we could plan our late-night raid. Just how he wanted to spend Christmas Eve.

Because McGoo had the uniform and the badge, he was the one who stepped up to the door of the Egyptian pyramid house. He pounded hard, knocking the festive wreath askew. It was long after midnight, but even the traffic on the main residential street was high, apparently for pre-Christmas Eve parties.

McGoo pounded again. "Mr. Eff-Tup, Saffron the Medusa—open up, this is the police. We have a warrant to search for stolen magical poultry."

Robin accompanied us, in case she needed to provide legal protection for her gorgon client. Sheyenne's spectral form drifted by my side, snuggling up even though we couldn't feel each other. Sometimes solving cases was the only kind of date we got to have.

The door opened, to reveal the white-wrapped Egyptian mummy. "We don't want any, it's late. You should be—" He looked at Officer McGoohan with his badge and Robin with the search warrant. The Medusa came to the door smiling airily; now she had mistletoe entwined among the rosebud-stuffed serpents on her head. They seemed drugged; maybe too much eggnog.

"Good to see you again, Miss Deyer! Honey, invite them in for some cookies." She seemed oblivious to why the guests might be there.

The mummy tried to slam the door on us, but McGoo stuck his shoe in the way, then forced his way in. He propped the door wide open.

I said, "We have reason to believe that you might be harboring a kidnapped wish turkey."

"No wish turkeys here," said Eff-Tup.

"What about other turkeys?" McGoo asked. "Several have gone missing."

The mummy shrugged. "It's that time of the season."

From the back of the pyramid we heard the sounds of rattling cages, squawking noises. Ducking under the extremely angled walls, we barged through the kitchen door to see a pyramid-shaped utility shed. Through mesh windows we heard more noises from inside, birds and other creatures.

"I need my lawyer," the mummy cried.

"Go ahead and call him. I have a warrant."

Behind the first storage unit was a tiny, stuffy corral that held a hobbled unicorn, filthy and skeletal, its mane and tail drooping and tangled. The creature's eyes were forlorn and sad, with less than ten feet of space to plod back and forth. The corral was filled with bright purple lumps of unicorn manure, each one sprouting pink flowers. When the unicorn snorted miserably, small rainbows came out of its nose.

"This is disgusting!" McGoo said.

"We kept it for its own good," said Saffron. "We were going to make the world full of magic and light."

Hearing the commotion from next door, Kashewpetl stormed over in his lurching stiff-jointed gait and shouted through the wide-open front door. "What's going on here?"

"In the back, Mr. Kashewpetl," I called. "I think we found your wish turkey."

Sheyenne went to comfort the poor unicorn and untie it.

Eff-Tup stood in front of the pyramidal storage unit, barring our way. "You'll never break the lock!" he insisted. It was secured with a simple hook-and-eye clasp. Did no one understand security these days?

McGoo easily flipped the hook.

Behind us, the Aztec mummy barged and took one look at the pyramid utility shed, furious. "Right here? My own neighbors? After I wish for my special sled, I'll never let you use it!"

"We're going to wish for world peace instead," said Saffron, "as soon as we get around to sacrificing the turkey."

McGoo swung open the flimsy door to reveal a shed of horrors—and not nice ones. We saw cages and cages of rescued, and then imprisoned, magical creatures. A trio of magic flower fairies huddled in gloom, looking brown and neglected, as if they hadn't been watered or fertilized in days. A multicolored feathered serpent was all scales and bones. Even a sullen, small lawn gnome hunched down in a cage much too small for it, so that its perky pointed cap was crumpled under the wire-mesh enclosure. "Help us," he moaned.

"Ugh," McGoo said, glowering at the Egyptian mummy and the Medusa. "There's nothing worse than incompetent do-gooders."

"We meant well!" Saffron said.

Then I spotted the turkey sporting Aztec ceremonial tattoos and golden bangles around its feet. "Here, Mr. Kashewpetl!"

The Aztec mummy stormed forward as best he could with his petrified joints. "That's my turkey! It's *my* wish! *I* get to sacrifice it! I want my sled!"

"That turkey's just a pawn," Robin said to me.

Even in this less-than-ostentatious cage, the turkey seemed fat and happy, without a care in the world. Kashewpetl flung the wire door wide, kicked the cage, rattled it. "Get out of there! Let's go home—up to the altar. It's Christmas Eve!"

The turkey squawked and fluttered out of the cage, its body so huge it could barely step forward, but it waddled out as if it were some sort of feathered Aztec god.

"You will not take our wonderful creatures!" And suddenly the peacenik Medusa seemed as fierce as one might expect a gorgon to be. Her eyes blazed bright, and her serpent hair writhed and flashed. But the snakes were all blindfolded and they couldn't get their fangs free of the rosebuds.

Eff-Tup threw himself on Kashewpetl, and the two mummies wrestled, in a rather stiff and slow-motion fashion. They fell against the cages, knocking the groaning lawn gnome off to the side.

"Careful! You'll break something!" shouted Kashewpetl.

"I intend to!" Eff-Tup said.

I found an empty plastic grocery bag hanging on a hook next to an unused unicorn pooper-scooper. I dumped the bag and yanked it over the Medusa's head, just in case those snakes figured a way out. McGoo easily pulled the mummies apart without tearing too many bandages.

During the tussle, though, the wish turkey flapped its wings, gobbled—and then bolted. It was too fat to run quickly, but we were preoccupied and didn't notice until it had already waddled through the pyramid house and sprinted out the open front door.

"Get the turkey!" I said, and suddenly we were all running.

All the pell-mell pursuers only made the turkey bolt faster. Gobbling, it ran into the busy street.

"Catch it!" Kashewpetl wailed so loudly that four moths came out of his lungs. "My sled!"

Saffron finally tore the plastic bag from her head. "World peace!" she cried.

The turkey waddled at full speed out into the street, and the gold bangles on its feet tripped it up—right as a delivery truck cruised by, well above the speed limit. The turkey looked up, caught the headlights. We all shouted in unison.

The truck honked its horn ... then rolled right over the turkey. With a loud squawk and a spray of feathers, it turned into flattened roadkill, all its bones smashed flat—including, no doubt, the wishbone.

The delivery truck screeched to a halt, and the zombie driver swung out, indignant. We all rushed to the scene, crowding around the truck. I recognized the driver. "Steve!"

He pulled down his cap and looked at me, deeply upset. "Now that's a fine Christmas Eve present! I wish you all would look both ways before crossing the street!"

Suddenly, the smashed wish turkey glowed, and as Robin, Sheyenne, and I stood together with McGoo, the two mummies, and Saffron the Medusa, we all felt the irresistible compulsion to look to our right, then to our left, assuring ourselves it was safe to enter the street.

Kashewpetl wailed. "That was *my* wish!"

Steve came up to me. "Sorry I snapped at you, dirt-buddy. I know I was going too fast, especially in a residential area."

"What are you doing out here?" I asked.

"Residential delivery—and sweet overtime. Plenty of necromancers have moved out to the suburbs, thanks to the high rent in the Quarter." He turned to look at the flattened mass of meat and feathers and bones. "Great, I gotta hose that off tonight. I hope that wasn't someone's Christmas turkey dinner."

"No, it wasn't," I said.

The Aztec mummy hunched over the flattened bird, trying to extricate the wishbone, which had already been broken into multiple pieces. "I wish I could have it back. I wish I could have my wish! I wish I could have my sled!"

The Medusa plucked another piece of the wishbone. "I wish I could cure all roadkill turkeys."

But the wish turkey had already exhausted its power, and none of their wishes came true.

McGoo stepped to Eff-Tup, Kashewpetl, and Saffron. He looked angrier than I'd ever seen him. "I'm calling this in. I've only got one set of handcuffs, so don't make me decide how to use them. Right now, you're going to help us catalogue and free all of those magical creatures from those cages."

"That unicorn really needs to be taken care of," said Sheyenne.

Robin had already made a call. "The UQ Unhumane Society's on the way. They'll be taking charge of these creatures until we can assess them for care or treatment. I'm sure that gnome is going to press charges, and I'm here to help expedite that."

I placed a commiserating arm around the hunched shoulders of the Aztec mummy. "I did find your missing turkey, Mr. Kashewpetl. I'm sorry it didn't turn out the way we would have liked."

"There's always next Christmas," he said. "I've waited this long. Someday I'll get my sled back. I'll raise another wish turkey. And next Christmas Eve ..."

"If you have a wish turkey that grants whatever you want, why don't you just ask for Suzitoq back?" I asked.

He looked startled. "Good idea! I'll raise two wish

turkeys, sacrifice them both, snap their wishbones so that I can have Suzitoq back—and our sled."

"Sounds like a plan," I said.

Sheyenne drifted close to me. "I wish we could just have Christmas together, Beaux. You and me."

"In that case, Spooky," I said, "you don't need a magic turkey. I promise I'll make your wish come true."

Heartbreaker

I

The Medusa was wearing a paper bag on her head when she entered Chambeaux & Deyer Investigations. Thank heavens for small miracles.

Sheyenne, our receptionist (and also my beautiful girlfriend) was the first to see her, but because Sheyenne is a ghost, she didn't have to worry about being turned to stone by the monstrous serpent-coiffed female.

I was in my office behind the desk, studying a pending case where a client had hired me to find a stolen interdimensional outhouse he used to reduce his sewage bill by transporting waste elsewhere. When a jealous neighbor used the privy without properly adjusting the dimensional outflow ports, the shit had really hit the fan.

With my door partway open, I heard someone enter from the hall, and Sheyenne cheerfully greeted the potential new client. "Hello, how may I help—oh!"

Here in the Unnatural Quarter, a startled reaction is

often the norm upon meeting someone, or something. I worked a calm smile on my undead face and stepped out of the office to make myself available. But Sheyenne yelped a warning. "Beaux! Be careful!"

I was transfixed—not because the Medusa was so hideous, but because the sight was just damned odd. The Medusa had a beautiful curvaceous body in a slinky sequined dress that reminded me of what Sheyenne had once worn as a lounge singer. I may be a zombie, but I'm still a male, so my attention was automatically drawn to the strange woman's ample cleavage. Before the Medusa could say, "Hey, my eyes are up here!" I saw that she had a brown paper bag covering her entire head.

Two small holes had been cut in the front of the bag so she could see, and seven larger breathing holes had been chewed through various parts of the paper. Hissing and bobbing snakes emerged through those holes, vipers with flicking tongues and long fangs. As the Medusa stood in front of Sheyenne's desk, the snakes weaved about, looking around. I was reminded of a dog sticking his head out of a car window and lolling his tongue into the breeze.

"I need an attorney," said the Medusa. "I'm fighting for my rights."

Words like that automatically attracted my lawyer partner Robin Deyer. As if summoned by a spell, she popped out of her office, trim and professional, ready to get down to business. She wore a fine business suit and carried a yellow legal pad and its accompanying magic pencil, ready to take notes. "We're happy to help you," Robin said, then froze next to me as she stared at the new arrival. To her credit, she looked at the Medusa's bag-covered head first, then let her gaze drop down to the cleavage and the rest of the well-formed body.

"My name is Alexandra, and I'm a Medusa. You'll have to take my word for it, because if I take this bag off my head, we won't have much more business together."

"Please don't," Sheyenne said quickly. "Company policy."

Alexandra adjusted the paper bag, gave the serpents on the top of her head room to move. "Is there someplace we can talk? I need to explain my case."

Robin and I led her into the conference room. Sheyenne floated after us with the proper intake paperwork. My girl-friend is an excellent receptionist and office manager, but I noticed that in this case she pointedly did not offer coffee, tea, or water for fear that Alexandra might lift up the bag in order to take a drink.

The Medusa was already fuming, having arrived in a pre-pissed-off state, and the snakes in her hair were simi-larly annoyed. "It's discrimination, pure and simple," she snapped, taking one of the conference room chairs, crossing one shapely leg over the other. "And I'm tired of it!" The serpents waved about and spat in agreement. "I'm a beautiful person, even though you can't see it with your own eyes."

If her head matched her body, then Alexandra was indeed gorgeous, but I didn't want to find out for myself. If I turned to stone because I gawked at another woman, Sheyenne would tell me I got what I deserved.

The Medusa continued, "I applied to enter the Miss

Unnatural beauty pageant, which is being held in just a few days at the Unnatural Quarter Community Center." She drummed her exquisitely manicured fingernails on the table. "The contest says: 'Beauty comes in all forms,' yet the rules explicitly exclude Medusas from entering. My entire race is forbidden. How is that not discrimination?"

Robin was indignant, as I had known she would be. "It's clearly not fair, but I've never actually been a fan of beauty pageants. They're exploitative and emphasize the wrong attributes for a successful woman."

"The winners do get wonderful sponsorship packages and a scholarship," Alexandra pointed out. "And I want the validation that I'm beautiful. There's no reason I should be forbidden from entering."

A detective's first weapon is to state the obvious. "It does seem unfair. If they allow werewolves, vampires, zombies, and banshees to enter, why not a Medusa? Didn't the Big Uneasy change the rules across the world when all the monsters came back? This is another set of rules that needs to be changed."

Alexandra turned her paper bag toward me, and I quickly averted my eyes, just in case. "Thank you, Mr. Chambeaux." The fact that she used my actual name rather than calling me "Shamble" earned her more brownie points in my book.

The Medusa leaned across the table, concentrating on Robin. "You don't see many Medusas out and about, because we have to live in the shadows. We're shunned. We need to stay hidden, even though we're contributing members of society. But I'm tired of hiding!" She pounded the table with her fist. "I can't get my hair done at a salon like everyone else, so I have to do home perms. Do you know how difficult that is, with these snakes in the way all the time?" She batted the top of her head, and the serpents playfully bit her hand but didn't puncture the skin. "I can't go out to a bar to find the love of my life. I can't stop to pick up milk at the grocery store without getting a paper bag like this—and now they're charging me a nickel a bag unless I bring one of my reusables with me."

Robin's rich brown eyes hardened. Once she goes on a crusade for justice, you don't want to get in her way. "You can't be discriminated against because of who you are. This problem is much more pervasive than a beauty pageant, but suing the pageant can be a springboard for a larger societal change."

Alexandra held out her well-manicured hands. "We have to start somewhere. I want to sue the contest officials, force them to change the rules so I can enter. I'm smart and witty and talented. I am beautiful, and I want the world to know it." Her raspy voice faltered as the emotions welled up inside her. "Can you help me, Ms. Deyer? Please?"

"Absolutely," Robin said. "This case could generate a lot of negative publicity, and the pageant committee wouldn't like that. Their sponsors sure wouldn't. Maybe we can knuckle them under with some strong language and a well-worded threat."

A sense of pride seemed to flow through her entire body, Alexandra seemed energized and confident. "Thank you! You'll change my life, and the lives of Medusas everywhere."

Robin looked down at the words written on her yellow legal pad. "I'll get on this right away, Alexandra. The pageant is coming up in a few days."

II

Since the case of the dangerously beautiful Medusa didn't require the services of a zombie detective, I was free to go out to lunch. Ready for a break, Sheyenne accompanied me to the Ghoul's Diner. She called it a date.

As a ghost, she doesn't need to eat and rarely breaks for lunch. Zombies don't need to eat much either, but I saw lunch as a business opportunity, a place to rub elbows with other monsters and chat up potential clients. When I sat at the diner counter with Sheyenne, I considered it a worthwhile outing, even though the food was always terrible.

Because many monsters are nocturnal, and others have little sense of time (being immortal), there's no such thing as a lunch rush. Instead, you can always find a random assortment of creatures who come in for their first disappointing experience or, for whatever incomprehensible reason, keep coming back.

Werewolves with trucker hats, zombies who smelled even worse than the food they were eating, and a handful of daring or befuddled humans sat at tables or along the stained counter. On the end stool, an old troll diligently worked on the newspaper's crossword puzzle, stymied because he wrote in runes rather than a normal alphabet. Esther, the harpy waitress, shrieked at the customers and pointedly demanded they leave at least a twenty percent tip, if they knew what was good for them.

A group of unnatural women in fancy dresses, stiletto heels, and too much makeup sat chatting around two pushed-together tables. I recognized the ladies of the night from the Full Moon brothel having a business lunch. At the head of the table, sitting like a piece of bandage-wrapped driftwood was Neffi, the ancient Egyptian madam who ran the semi-legal brothel with an iron-hard and sinewy hand as well as a real heart of stone. I had been there many times, though not as a customer (Sheyenne made sure of that); Neffi had once hired me as a P.I. and outside security when fighting off some unsavory racketeers who were trying to move in to the Quarter.

As Sheyenne and I pondered the disappointing menu selections, Esther came up from behind the counter with a face that looked as pinched as a finger caught in a door-jamb. She slammed down a bitter cup of coffee, turned around to the shelf under the heat lamps, grabbed whatever plate happened to be available, and clattered it in front of me.

"I know what you're going to order, Dan Shamble." She spun to Sheyenne with a vain attempt at a smile. "And what do you need, hon?"

"Just a cup of hot water." When she smiled, her translucent glow lit up the place. "I like to inhale the vapors."

"Hot water costs as much as real tea," Esther warned. "Because of my time and effort."

I interrupted what was sure to become a contentious lecture. "That's fine, Esther."

"You always know how to be a good customer, Shamble." The waitress flounced off to annoy other customers.

Sheyenne snuggled closer, though I couldn't feel her ghostly presence. She looked around the crowded diner, listening to the buzz of conversation, the clatter of plates. Back in the kitchen, Albert the ghoul proprietor stumbled around, dripping and leaking bodily fluids into dishes in the sink and pots on the stove. Whatever emerged from the pots ended up on the plates, and the customers knew not to complain. Fortunately, my senses of smell and taste were permanently dulled.

Sheyenne said, "Since our caseload is light, I'll use the time to catch up on paperwork. A good filing system makes me happy."

I was glad that I didn't have to do the filing myself. "It's one of the many things I love about you, Spooky."

When I'd first met her, Sheyenne worked as a cocktail waitress and singer at the Basilisk nightclub, until she'd been poisoned to death, and when I tried to investigate the murder, I'd gotten myself killed, too. Fortunately, thanks to all of the changes the Big Uneasy had made in the world, death didn't mean that our relationship had to end. A zombie and ghost were a bit of an odd couple, I admit, but we made it work.

Sheyenne slowly inhaled the steam that wafted up from her cup of hot water. The lunch special squirmed and burbled on my plate, but I hadn't dared to touch it yet.

The girls from the Full Moon brothel let out a round of laughter. Considering their good mood, I guessed that Neffi was picking up the lunch tab. They discussed interesting new techniques for various species of customers while Neffi scribbled down suggested price changes. I saw sleek-looking werewolf women, classy vampire ladies, even a cold and well-preserved female zombie who was apparently quite popular during Necrophilia Night. Neffi, though withered and ancient, had been quite a dish in her day, and now she drank large glasses of special herb infusions to rehydrate her desiccated flesh.

The madam made eye contact with me and flashed her exposed teeth. She waved a stick-like hand at me, then rose to amble up to the counter. "Dan Shamble, what a delight to see you! Why haven't you come to visit us at the Full Moon? We miss you there." Neffi leaned closer and said seductively, "All the ladies miss you."

Sheyenne's aura turned a brighter blue. "He doesn't need your services. I give him everything he wants."

"Of course you do, dear." Neffi patted the beautiful ghost on the stool next to me, but her hand passed right through the intangible form. "Your sweetheart made it perfectly clear that our relationship is strictly business, nothing romantic or sexual." She cackled. "I keep telling him what he's missing, but he doesn't believe me."

At the table, the other unnatural ladies waved and made flirtatious smiles. Cinnamon, the ginger-furred werewolf blew me a kiss with her muzzle. Fortunately, the embalming fluid keeps my skin at a monotone so Sheyenne didn't see me flush in embarrassment.

"We're at a business lunch to discuss our caseload," I said.

Neffi clucked her wood-dry tongue against her ivory

teeth. "I wanted to drop some business your way." She leaned closer. "It's about the competition, and I don't like it one bit."

I was surprised to hear about another brothel in the Quarter. "The Full Moon has competition?"

"Oh, not another brothel." Neffi rattled out a sound of disgust. "The Internet. A new unnaturals-only dating service just launched, and it's extremely successful. You may have heard of it: Monster Match."

I remembered their jingles from the radio. Monster Match was a special service for Very Lonely Hearts, where unnaturals of all kinds could connect with compatible personalities and biological types. "Sounds perfectly legitimate. It's just a dating service."

"Just a dating service!" Neffi repeated with a huff. Her bones rattled and creaked within her dried wrappings. "The Full Moon is the obvious and legitimate place for horny unnaturals. Why do they need to sign up for a dating service?"

"Maybe they're actually lonely and looking for a soulmate?" Sheyenne suggested.

"That's what we offer! Soulmates by the hour. What could be more economical?"

Before the conversation could escalate, I raised a hand. "I can look into them, Neffi, but there's probably nothing I can do if Monster Match is a legal business."

The mummy madam sulked. "You're sure there's no way you can go break some kneecaps?"

"I'm pretty sure broken kneecaps are out of the question."

Neffi sighed. "Do what you can. We'll pay your regular rate ... or we can work out a trade if you stop off at the Full Moon." She cackled, and the girls at the table all waved at me again.

Sheyenne said in a sour voice, "If Beaux can do anything for you, I'll send you a bill."

III

Quiet days may be boring, but they're much better than getting shot at or having limbs torn off by angry monsters (yes, I have had those kinds of days). At the end of a slow afternoon, I headed off to the Goblin Tavern to sit at my usual bar stool and have my usual warm flat beer with my Best Human Friend, Officer Toby McGoohan, also known as McGoo. I arrived just in time for the start of Unhappy Hour.

The Goblin Tavern is a fixture in the Quarter, a regular hangout for monsters of all sorts, including zombie detectives and beat cops who've been transferred here because they couldn't get along with their human coworkers. The Goblin Tavern is a place where everybody knows your name and doesn't hold it against you.

McGoo sat on his regular stool. He's a beat cop, dressed in the usual UQPD blue uniform and cap. He supposedly works regular hours, though I could never figure out what they were. He always seemed to be around, often when I needed him, often when we needed a drink.

"Hey, Shamble," he said as I walked through the door.

The light inside the tavern was dim, but so was the light outside, so my eyes adjusted quickly.

Four vampire teenagers stood around the pool table, taking care to use plastic cues rather than the more dangerous pointed wooden variety. Two zombies of the rotting-and-falling-apart sort attempted to throw darts at the dartboard but managed to hit only the floor or each other. A zombie hurled a dart so hard that one of his fingers came off. The tumbling finger hit the bullseye, while the dart thumped against the wall.

Francine the salty bartender was a woman in her late fifties with a complexion going on 100, but she covered it with enough makeup to look like a teenager on prom night. Seeing me enter, she automatically swung toward the beer taps and began filling a mug for me. McGoo grinned and patted the bar stool next to him. "All ready for you, Shamble."

It's nice to feel at home.

When I looked down, I saw he had placed a pink plastic bladder on the wooden seat, a painfully obvious whoopee cushion. "You expect me to sit on that?"

"Just wanted to relieve a little pressure. You seem to be outgassing all the time anyway." He chuckled and took a long slurp of his beer.

Francine set my mug in front of me. "Anything dangerous going on in the Quarter, Mr. Shamble?"

"Nothing much to worry about today." I looked up at the TV, where a commercial for this year's Miss Unnatural pageant caught my attention. The cheap advertisement flashed pictures of foxy werewolves, zombies, or vampire women wearing sparkly gowns, special jewelry, even scanty swimsuits that revealed a lot of fur, pale skin, or scales, something for everyone. "Beauty comes in all forms!" said the commercial.

I used my beer mug to point at the TV. "We just got a client connected to that contest, but it's a legal thing, discrimination case with a Medusa. Robin's on it. I've got a light caseload."

McGoo drank his beer, pondering. "Hey, Shamble, what's a Medusa's favorite cheese?"

I didn't see the trap. "I don't know, what's a Medusa's favorite cheese?"

"Gorgonzola!"

I didn't even groan. "You must have had a quiet day, too, if you have time to think up dumb jokes like that."

"Walking my beat gives me plenty of time to think," McGoo replied. "Right now I don't have any urgent cases, just the usual missing persons."

"Seems like there are always missing persons around the Quarter," I said.

McGoo put his elbows on the bar. "I don't understand how monsters can misplace themselves so often. We've been getting reports of young unnatural men vanishing, but not the usual seedy types. These are quiet, single, upstanding males, no criminal record—shy, nerdy types. Ten of them disappeared in the past couple of weeks." He slurped his beer again, and I saw I needed to hurry if I was going to catch up. "Since we have so many missing unnaturals, I think we should start a Lost-and-Found Department rather than Missing Persons."

"Send me the files of the missing young men and I'll keep an eye out for them," I said. I put my elbows on the bar and drank my beer, just like him. "I don't have much going on right now."

"Good." McGoo raised his now-empty mug to get Francine's attention. "Then you have time to buy me a second round."

IV

When the shouting started in the meeting, the members of the Miss Unnatural pageant committee were loud enough to make you wish you knew how to spell the word "cacophony."

Robin had set up the meeting at our offices for the day after we had met the Medusa, summoning the pageant committee on threat of legal action. Those last five words usually provoked an immediate response. Our new client wore a different sequined cocktail gown and a fresh paper bag on her head. This time, Alexandra had used a large paper punch to cut perfect round holes for her eyes, as well as others for ventilation for her hair serpents.

The four members of the pageant committee also served as the panel of judges. Sheila was a blond-haired harpy whose disposition made PMS seem a delightful alternative. Her name had an intrinsic built-in shriek when she introduced herself as *Sheeeeeeee-ila!* She was a past Miss Unnatural herself, which made her arrogant and judgmental of the less-adequate contestants. Next to her sat a prim blue-haired old lady named Eleanor, who had her hair done up so perfectly that it took me a moment to realize she was a zombie.

Lewis, a dapper broad-shouldered werewolf with lush brown fur wore a pinstripe suit and seemed quite erudite and proper, like a butler who had inherited all of his master's wealth. The last committee member was a big gray golem with clay features, a smooth bare chest, and a round head like a basketball, with indentations for eyes. He was the quietest of the four, but when he spoke his words came out in a deep rumbling voice. He was either keenly interested or just a lump of soft rock. His name was Egnort.

The pageant committee arrived at 1:00 sharp, responding to the summons that Robin insisted was merely a "polite invitation." After Sheyenne led them into the conference room, Lewis got down to business before they even sat down. "We have a great deal of work to finish before the pageant tomorrow night. What is this all about?"

"Legal action!" shrieked Sheila. "How dare you threaten legal action! We run a clean contest! Even I was Miss UQ! The pageant's reputation is flawless, just ask any of our sponsors!"

"Lots of pretty ladies," Egnort muttered as he slumped into the groaning chair.

They all noticed our client sitting at the far end of the table, glaring at them through the eye holes in the brown paper bag.

Robin made her case calmly, threatening to expose the obvious discrimination in court before a jury of unnatural peers. In a normal, rational world, the committee would have seen the error of their ways, but the world hadn't been rational since the Big Uneasy changed all the rules of magic and monsters. On the other hand, I didn't recall the world ever being normal and rational, with or without monsters.

Sheila's shriek was loud enough to rattle the windows in the conference room. Lewis growled deep in his throat, and the golem shook the whole table by pounding with his hefty fist. The blue-haired old zombie lady made no noise whatsoever, but I'm sure she was thinking unkind thoughts.

Sheyenne hovered next to me, worried, and she whispered in my ear, "It's all right, Beaux. I had them sign the glass-breakage disclaimer."

With monster tempers flaring, I was more worried about Robin-breakage than glass breakage.

Alexandra rose to her feet and all her serpents stood erect, hissing. Muffled by the paper bag, she said, "But I am beautiful! I want people to see me. I want people to judge me as the most beautiful woman in the Quarter! You can't discriminate against my entire race!"

"It's a clear case of bias," Robin said, gently urging the Medusa to sit back down. "None of you can argue with that. It doesn't matter how beautiful Alexandra is, as long as she thinks she has a chance. It's her right."

"Let me show you how beautiful I am!" Alexandra grabbed the paper bag, but Robin nearly tackled her, tugging the covering back in place. Sheila and Eleanor quickly averted their eyes, and Lewis howled. The golem just sat there grinning with his big clay lips.

"Calm down," I said. "We're talking about a beauty pageant. No need for this to get ugly."

Robin picked up her yellow legal pad and tapped the pencil on the notes. "The law is clear in matters like this, I'm afraid. The rules of your pageant prevent Alexandra from being a contestant for no other reason than who she is. No jury in the world would disagree with us."

I didn't point out that any jury would be turned to stone if Alexandra ever testified.

Eleanor explained in a thin church-lady voice, "We also exclude males as a general class of contestants. Is that discriminatory, too, Ms. Deyer?"

"And hermaphrodites," Lewis added. "As well as genderless nonsexual entities."

Egnort sounded disappointed. "That's why you don't see any golem contestants."

"Do they even make female golems?" I wondered aloud.

Egnort used his big hands to rearrange his chest to produce a remarkable pair of breasts. "Depends on where you squish the clay."

"Thanks," I said, "I didn't need to see that."

"Medusas have rights!" Alexandra insisted. "This is why I hired Ms. Deyer."

All four judges were clearly exasperated. "Talk all you like about rights, miss, but what does it *mean*?" Sheila cried. "Even if we allowed her on stage, what is a Medusa going to do during the bikini contest?"

Robin made a disgusted sound. "The bikini contest is intrinsically exploitative."

The old zombie lady calmly explained, "This isn't a theoretical question, Ms. Deyer. We have to exclude Medusas for reasons of public safety. In a similar rule, we cannot allow banshees to compete in the singing contest. It's just too dangerous."

"Public safety is paramount," Lewis said.

Alexandra's snakes twitched and hissed. Behind the brown paper bag, I knew the Medusa must be wearing a very pissy expression.

Robin remained indignant. "You'd better find some accommodation for my client to compete just like any other unnatural." She reached over to give the Medusa's wrist a reassuring pat. "Put up gauzy curtains or filmy screens, something to decrease the stone potency, but which will still allow her to be a contestant."

"How can we do that?" shrieked Sheila. "The contest is tomorrow night!" The other committee members shifted uncomfortably.

"You'd better think fast," I said.

V

The unnatural beauty contest got me thinking about the quiet, nerdy young men on McGoo's missing persons / lost-and-found list, and that made me remember Neffi's complaints about the Monster Match dating service. It occurred to me that lonely monster singles would be more likely to sign up for a dating service than venture into the frightening unnatural singles-bar scene or a brothel, no matter how many coupons Neffi gave out.

While Robin furiously filed motions, sent angry letters, and did incomprehensible legal jousting (give me my .38 or a good fistfight any day) on the Medusa's behalf, I had Sheyenne look up the address for Monster Match. Then I quickly explained that I didn't intend to sign up as a client.

The dating service headquarters was a room not much larger than a broom closet, a small rented spot in a larger office building. Many such services would have been nothing more than a "suite number," which really meant a P.O. Box in a shipping store. Monster Match was a real, physical space with a receptionist, a manager, and an in-house data specialist. All three were the same person, a short balding human with a round head, a round face, a round nose, and a round belly.

He smiled politely up at me as I stepped into the cramped office. I barely had enough room to close the door behind me with only two feet of space between the door and the desk of the receptionist/manager/IT guy.

"Welcome to Monster Match!" he said, sizing me up, noting my fedora, my grayish skin, the bullet hole in my forehead, the stitched-up sports jacket. "I'm so glad you came in person. Our new clients are often shy, but I can assure you we have many fine matches, many lovely zombie women, or other unnaturals?" He raised his eyebrows, which made his naked forehead wrinkle all the way to the top of his head. "If you're more adventurous, we have other types as well, same sex, same species, same level of decay. Something for everyone." Before I could stop him, he pulled out a clipboard with a new application form. He introduced himself as Terry Bookings.

I cut him off by showing him my private investigator's license. "I'm just here doing a little investigation." I handed him a business card, which he studied carefully.

"Hmm, still sounds exciting. Are you single? A zombie private investigator would look great on your profile."

"I'm already romantically haunted. This is strictly business." I tried to explain in a way that didn't contain too many lies or exaggerations. "I often assist the UQPD in some of their missing-persons investigations, and I'm also trying to head off a potential business dispute between you and the Full Moon brothel."

Terry Bookings frowned. "Oh, I wouldn't go near a place like that. I prefer my dates to be safe, distant electronic contact. Most of our clients are shy, especially the members of our gold-level Very Lonely Hearts Club."

That sounded strange. "Monster Match doesn't arrange actual dates in person?"

"Oh, only in our elite packages. Many clients are too shy to do anything but interact on social media or by email. Eventually, though, some of them find the nerve to venture out of the shadows and meet their soul mates."

"This might be a stretch, but a string of young men from exactly that demographic have gone missing in the Quarter." I explained what McGoo had told me in the Goblin Tavern. "They were all quiet, single, and lived alone."

"Precisely our clientele." Bookings grinned. "But such people aren't exactly rare. You'd be surprised how many lonely monsters there are. It's all about finding the right person, and Monster Match expedites that process. With so many terrifying things in the world, the most terrifying thing of all is finding the right soul mate."

I was curious about this man and his motivations. "Are you married yourself, Mr. Bookings? Do you have a certain special partner?" I wondered if his own soul mate was human like himself, or something else entirely.

Switching to his IT and database-management persona, Bookings patted the computer keyboard behind him. "I have my database."

I kept taking mental notes. "I'm surprised a human would run a dating service for unnaturals. What drew you to romance and monsters?" There was nothing particularly suspicious about that. Robin, too, had set up shop in the Quarter because she wanted justice for all monsters, and I had come here as a human detective—when I was still alive—because I'd seen a good business opportunity.

"Every heart needs love, whether or not it's still beating," said Bookings. "This was an untapped niche market, a very big niche ... a bottomless pit, in fact. The natural world already has highly specialized dating services that help people find hookups among their chosen set—sanitation workers only, butchers only, bankers only, manicurists only. So why not monsters only? Monster Match has been amazingly successful, if only unnaturals would stop being so shy."

"Maybe you can check your list of clients?" I pulled out the names of the ten missing persons McGoo had told me about. "Just to see if there's any connection. We need to find these people."

Now Bookings became stern. "We have privacy concerns and confidentiality issues, Mr. Chambeaux. I am not allowed to reveal the names of my clients."

Robin had taught me that you can always find a loophole. "Maybe you could just check them out yourself while I fill out this form?" I took the clipboard from him. "If you don't see anything odd, then you don't have to tell me."

I saw no place to sit down, or barely even turn around in the closet-sized office, so I stepped back six inches and leaned against the wall. I used the pen on the clipboard to start filling in my name. Bookings struggled with the idea, and then went into his IT-specialist persona. Looking at the names on the missing-persons list, he began to scroll through his client database. I wasn't sure he would tell me anything, but I reminded myself this had been a long shot no matter what.

I'd barely finished writing my name in the first line of the form before Bookings muttered in surprise as he checked one after another on the Monster Match listings. "Hmmm, these are indeed clients, Mr. Chambeaux. All ten of them." He pulled up more details of the profiles, sounding quite concerned. I was relieved not to fill out the rest of the form.

"All ten are gold-level clients, the ones who got up the nerve to request a real in-person date. That's quite rare." He pulled up profile after profile. "Young vampire men, mummies, werewolves, ghouls." When I leaned closer, he hunched his shoulders so I couldn't see details on the screen.

"We set them up with their perfect match, a lonely unnatural female who hit all their special criteria." Bookings shook his head. "But after the dates, they never bothered to post a review. Do you know how impossible it is to get your clients to post a review?" He sounded exasperated. "That's always been a problem. I mean, how difficult is it to go on the site, type a few sentences, give us five stars? It means a lot to our business, but they just don't care." He huffed. "And after their one in-person date, none of those ten renewed their weekly membership. Not a one!" He sighed. "I do wish I could have helped those Very Lonely Hearts find romance. I wonder what went wrong."

With all ten missing young men connected with Monster Match, that was a clue even a zombie detective couldn't ignore. "And who were their dates with? Is there any connection? Maybe she ... or he, or it knows something."

"I can't tell you that!" Bookings sounded indignant, but I had piqued his curiosity. "I couldn't possibly ..." He kept muttering about privacy concerns as he dug into his database, clicking from one profile to the next, and he grew visibly more alarmed as he read one after another. "Hmmm, they all went on a first date with the same young woman." He swallowed hard. "I admit that's quite a coincidence."

"Tell me who it is," I demanded, without adding a question mark at the end of my sentence.

"I couldn't, I really couldn't." He seemed very nervous.

Suspicions were already forming in my mind. "Can you at least tell me what species she is?"

He fumbled with his lip, stared at the screen, tried to block the view, and finally admitted, "It's a Medusa. They all dated a Medusa."

"Alexandra," I said.

He quailed, covering the screen with his palms. "I didn't tell you that!"

"You didn't have to," I said.

"And I'm not giving you her address. That would be unethical."

"No need." I bumped against the wall in my rush to squeeze back out of the doorway. I already had Alexandra's address in the Chambeaux & Deyer client paperwork. I needed to contact McGoo.

VI

I don't usually concern myself with the dating habits of supernatural creatures, but the Medusa connection was sufficient cause for alarm. Once I learned where Alexandra lived, presumably the place where shy but hopeful lonely-hearts monster singles picked her up for their dates, I called for backup—McGoo. In fact, since this was UQPD business, I decided I would use him as more than backup, but rather send him right up front.

By the time we converged near Alexandra's home, it was late afternoon. I didn't know what the Medusa did for a living, though it had to be something safely out of sight, probably an online business. Whatever it was, Alexandra did rather well for herself, considering the size of her villa in the suburbs.

The home had Grecian architecture with decorative marble pillars out front next to the mailbox. A wide burbling fountain added class to the front yard, although the cheery pink lawn flamingoes seemed incongruous. High hedges formed an impenetrable wall so we couldn't see the back yard. A quaint gate that looked as if it had been designed by a children's fantasy illustrator led through the hedge into the back.

"This is the kind of villa I'm going to have on the Mediterranean coast when I retire," McGoo said.

"I hope you started saving for that a few lifetimes ago." We stepped up to the arched front door between more fancy marble columns. Next to the doorbell, an ominous-looking plaque warned *Solicitors Will Be Turned to Stone.* I realized it wasn't an empty threat.

When I rang the doorbell, a clear crystalline chime reverberated through the villa. I backed away, yanking the fedora down over my face for protection. I hissed to McGoo, "Avert your eyes when she answers the door! I can't deal with a dangerous Medusa and a petrified cop at the same time."

"I've seen the warnings on the commercials," McGoo said. "You're supposed to call a doctor if you stay rock-hard for more than three hours."

When no one answered, I rang the doorbell again, and we stood waiting awkwardly on the front porch, listening to the fountain trickle. So much for a dramatic confrontation.

"Usually, the apprehension of a suspect is more exciting than this," McGoo said. "How long do you think we should wait? Should we leave a note on the door?"

We heard a rustling in the hedges nearby, then a gruff male voice said, "I'm here in the back, working in the garden. Come 'round to the gate."

Leaving the front porch, we walked along a flagstone path to the low, rounded wooden door designed for either hobbits or Pooh-bears. The gate swung open, and we saw something else out of a children's fantasy illustration. A bent dwarf in a floppy red hat and red vest, brown pants, black boots with a bright buckle on each foot. A long gray beard sprouted from his chin, and his eyes shrunken, squinted into a nest of wrinkles, obviously blind.

"Heigh-ho?" The dwarf sniffed the air with an overlong nose and squinted closer to us, unable to see. "Who is it?" He leaned on his garden spade, then wiped his dirty hands off on his pants. "Are you here to see Mistress Alexandra?"

"Yes, I'm Dan Chambeaux, private investigator, and she's one of our clients. This is Officer McGoohan from the UQ Police Department. We have a few questions for her."

"She's not here right now. I'm just the gardener, Putter." He sniffed. "I wouldn't mind the company, though."

"Putter?" McGoo asked. "Because you like to putter around out back?"

The dwarf squinched his face in a scowl. "No, because I like to golf, but I'm no good at it since going blind. I hit the ball, then I spend an hour feeling around to find it. These days I pretty much stay on the putting green."

He swung open the gate and let us through the hedge into the back courtyard. "Come inside so I can keep working. I'm maintaining the mistress's statue garden."

That immediately put me on my guard. "A statue garden?"

"They're marvelous and lifelike," Putter said. "Mistress Alexandra is quite the collector, and I've made sure the new arrivals are properly arranged. Most importantly, I keep the bird shit off of them."

Inside, many of the shrubs were trimmed and shaped into interesting topiary animals. He led us past tulips and daffodils, snapdragons, and a large hungry-looking Venus flytrap. Ahead stood ten white marble figures of unnatural young men.

McGoo opened and closed his mouth. I didn't need to review the checklist of missing persons to know that each of these statues was one of the lonely nerds from Monster Match. There were vampires, werewolves, two reasonably well-preserved young zombies, a frog demon, a mummy, a ghoul. Each one of these would-be suitors had been turned to stone, their petrified expressions uplifted and smiling, showing how shy and hopeful they were to go on a date. Three even held bouquets of flowers in their hands, which had wilted away by now.

"That's what you call looking for love in all the wrong places," McGoo muttered.

Putter moved forward blindly, using the spade on the margin of the gravel path, bending over to pluck weeds. He pulled a rag out of his pocket and began polishing the statue of a young, mousy vampire who had puckered up and closed his eyes for a kiss, except he had taken a peek—a peek of the wrong thing, which turned him to stone.

"Now, what did you want to chat with the mistress about?" asked Putter. "I can't see the statues. How do they look? They feel very lifelike."

"Not lifelike anymore," McGoo said, then turned to me, "We'll need some blindfolded backup when Alexandra gets home. I'm calling the UQPD."

"Do you have any ghost cops on the force yet?" I asked. "They'd be immune to her powers."

"None yet, but a few rookies are in training. It's just you and me, Shamble."

I hardened my voice and turned to the blind dwarf. "We need to see Alexandra right now, Putter. Well, not exactly *see* her, but speak with her. It is a matter of great concern."

The gardener stopped at a plastic five-gallon pail filled with slimy chicken entrails. He tossed a handful to the snapping jaws of the Venus flytrap. "As I said, Mistress Alexandra isn't here. This is her big day. She's already gone."

I groaned. "Of course!"

"What's the matter, Shamble?" McGoo asked. "We've got to take her into custody before she hurts someone else."

"Oh, she'll have plenty of time to talk with you after the pageant," said Putter. "This is her big opening night on full stage at the Miss Unnatural contest." He grinned, even though he couldn't see anything. He leaned back against the statue of a hopeful-looking werewolf. "I bet she wins."

VII

If I hadn't been so busy tracking down monster dating services and missing unnatural persons, I would have realized that Sheyenne and Robin wanted to go to the Miss Unnatural pageant. Sheyenne always asserted that men are clueless.

Leaving Alexandra's fancy Greek-style villa and her ominous statue garden as full dark fell, McGoo and I raced to the UQ Community Center, where the gala pageant was being held. The community center was a spacious building that often hosted Bingo night for veteran monsters. Now, large spotlights shone up at the sky, swooping back-and-forth into the night like a test run for the Bat Signal. I knew they were actually rented from the spectacle of a shoe sale that had run the previous week.

We arrived in time to see a long line of sleek black limousines and sleek black hearses dropping off the last few celebrity guests, who strutted along the blood-red carpet. Gremlin paparazzi pestered them, carrying huge cameras, while younger paparazzi simply used their smartphones to post photos instantly on social media feeds.

"It's already started, McGoo," I said. We elbowed our way through the crowds of spectators. In my slouched fedora and stitched-up sport jacket and McGoo in his beat-cop uniform, we were woefully underdressed. "We don't have tickets. How are we going to get inside?"

He pulled out his badge. "I have a VIP pass." I copied

him and pulled out my P.I. license, hoping it would be good enough for at least a balcony seat.

The audience was filled with beautiful people, werewolf ladies with their fur coiffed in extravagant hairdos, polished ivory skeletons decked with so many pearls that they rattled and clattered as they walked. Mummies wore fresh linen bandages; vampire women had pale skin, crimson lips, and scarlet lacquered claws.

We grabbed programs from a stack on a table. Slick black-and-white pages of head shots of the contestants (at least the ones who showed up on film, while others had to settle for sketches), full-page ads from the main sponsors, pages of smaller ads from contestant sponsors and overly excited family members. McGoo thumbed through his program and smirked as we walked. I thought of all the beauty salons, the dress shops, the perfume makers and embalming parlors that the pageant kept in business. No wonder the judges had been intimidated by the threat of legal action. This was quite a racket.

Robin had demanded the contest work out some kind of accommodation for Alexandra, but now that I knew our client was a murderer, her rights as a contestant seemed less important. The Medusa would be locked up in a mirror-walled cell as soon as McGoo could figure out how to arrest her.

The doors were closed, but we needed to get inside before the Medusa unleashed whatever mayhem she intended.

McGoo has many talents and being rude is one of them. He used that talent now as he plowed his way toward the door with me shambling in his wake. "Police business! Make way!" he barked.

The last gawkers and spectators shuffled away as we barged up to the ticket window. A nearsighted female troll with cats-eye glasses looked down at her keyboard and the stack of Will Call envelopes. "I'm afraid the lights have gone down and the pageant has started." The troll ticket taker shook her head. "You'll need to be escorted." She pointed to a small warming shack near the main doors, where five listless zombies in tuxedoes stood around, waiting for something to do. "Go over there to the House of Usher. One of the ushers will take you inside."

After McGoo flashed his badge and I showed my P.I. license, a zombie usher led us through the door and quietly into the aisles as if he knew where we were going, and McGoo and I followed as if we believed him. I thought Robin and Sheyenne would be sitting up very close to the front.

The community center looked full, every seat occupied, and all faces were turned forward, staring at the spectacle. Ahead of us, the broad stage was framed with high, scalloped red velvet curtains and celebratory streamers. Under bright floodlights, gorgeous (depending on your definition) female contestants in swimsuits paraded across the front of the stage, some wearing bikinis, others in one-pieces. They strutted back and forth exuding confidence, some of them even transmitting glamour spells. One of the pale zombie women exposed her shriveled, pruned skin as if she had been submerged for a very long time. An aquatic female creature oozed slime, which made her skin glisten enticingly in the spotlights. Werewolves showed off their sleek belly fur. A vampire woman's fangs gleamed so brightly she had obviously smeared them with Vaseline.

"I don't see Alexandra," I whispered to McGoo.

"That's probably a good thing," McGoo cracked, his attention distracted by the beauty queens in spite of himself.

The zombie usher turned sideways and let out a wet, scolding, "*Sssssh!*"

The four judges sat at a long table on the side of the stage, Lewis the werewolf in his pinstripe suit, Eleanor the blue-haired zombie lady, Sheila the arrogant harpy and former contest winner, and the gray clay golem Egnort. The golem just stared at the women, while the other three judges took diligent notes, although it looked as if Lewis was working on a crossword puzzle.

The usher led us down the aisle toward the front, barely able to see the faint running lights. I spotted Robin in a reserved seat in the second row, and Sheyenne's spectral form drifted up the aisle toward us after she saw us coming. She swooped close, whispering, "Beaux, you made it!"

"Did Robin get Alexandra among the contestants?" I asked. "We've got to stop her from coming out on stage. She'll turn everybody to stone."

Sheyenne didn't seem concerned as we hurried toward the seats. The zombie usher had trouble keeping up with us. "Don't worry, Robin took care of that. The committee made protective accommodations, so everything's fine."

Looking exhausted, the zombie usher stopped at the

second row and extended a gray hand toward Robin and a pair of conveniently empty seats next to her. Sheyenne said, "We hoped you two would come, so we bought extra tickets."

The swimsuit contestants filed off the stage into the dim expanse behind the big velvet curtains as the orchestra played a fanfare. The announcer asked for a round of applause, which was politely given, accompanied by catcalls and werewolf whistles.

At stage left, waiting to give their solo singing performances according to the program, sat the vivacious unnatural ladies from the Full Moon brothel. Neffi wore a fine white linen gown over her freshly re-wrapped bandages as well as gaudy gold and scarab jewels. She and all of her ladies had entered, hoping for one of them to be crowned Miss Unnatural, and then she could charge a premium.

While McGoo and I squirmed forward to our seats, dodging knees covered by cocktail gowns and tuxedo pants, I kept a worried eye on the stage, not convinced I could believe Sheyenne's reassurances. When Robin motioned us to our seats, she seemed victorious and proud. "It's all been worked out. Alexandra will get her time in the limelight. She's on next, once they set up the screens."

I leaned close to Robin. "She'll also get her time in jail. That Medusa already murdered ten young men who signed up for the Monster Match dating service. She turned them to stone on the first date and stashed the statues back at her villa."

Robin looked horrified. "I'm sure it was an accident, and it can't happen here at the pageant. I was very specific in the accommodations." She pointed to the front of the auditorium where lurking stage hands rolled forward gauzy fabric screens on large wooden frames. When backlit from behind the stage, the silhouettes of the stage hands were razor sharp. "The fabric is thin, but it's been tested to be sufficient to filter out the Medusa's petrification spell. The judges and the audience can see Alexandra in great detail without being turned to stone. She's going to give an impassioned speech, classified as a dramatic talent entry."

As the stage was prepared for the Medusa, I looked uneasily at the huge folded curtains that had been raised above the stage, leaving heavy shadows in the back area and the usual theatrical debris: ladders, props, and push brooms, next to all the ropes that held up the scaffolding, the lighting, and the curtains.

While the judges waited, and the audience muttered impatiently, McGoo ground his teeth together, dissatisfied. "It's not as if Alexandra can get away, Shamble. We'll arrest her as soon as the pageant is over." He glanced at me in the seat beside him. "If we rush the stage now, you know what'll happen."

I nodded slowly. "Yeah, they'll try to crown me as Miss Unnatural."

McGoo snorted.

When the tall screens formed a barrier in front of the stage, the announcer boomed, "And now, our first ever Medusa contestant in the Miss Unnatural pageant! Give a round of applause for the fascinating and dangerous Alexandra!"

The orchestra played a spritely fanfare, and the audience made polite applause. The bright backlighting showed the slender, sexy figure outlined in perfect curvaceous silhouette and a serpentine hairdo that was at once horrifying and hypnotic. At least a part of me was desperate to see what her face actually looked like, but I hardened my resolve before her glance could harden my skin.

The Medusa approached the thin fabric on the screens, and Alexandra spoke in her sultry voice. "I am here to speak out for all the beautiful people that no one ever sees. Think of the unnatural women who live in the shadows, who hide their true selves because they don't want to be laughed at or embarrassed. This pageant is supposed to celebrate beauty in all forms! Throughout history, Medusas have been forced to hide, living in labyrinths, glimpsed only through mirrors. Tonight, at this beauty pageant, I've decided to come out in public."

The audience muttered their support. Many of them, especially the celebrity attendees, wore wristbands or lapel pins to promote prominent causes from days or weeks past. I sensed that new armbands and lapel pins would soon spring up across the Quarter for the *Beauty in All Forms* movement.

I uneasily watched her stark silhouette from behind the thin screen. From their table on the stage, the four judges watched as well through a filmy side screen. The golem sat straight-backed, his smooth gray face turned toward the seductive shape. The harpy Sheila scowled and snickered, but it seemed to be her normal expression. Eleanor paid close attention, nodding slowly. Bent over his folded newspaper, Lewis found the correct five-letter word that finished his crossword puzzle, and he looked up, immensely satisfied with himself.

Alexandra continued her inspirational talk. "I'm tired of being demonized as a woman, tired of being described as too ugly for anyone to look at. Who's to say I'm not too *beautiful*? Tonight, I'll show you just how beautiful I really am."

The audience was transfixed by her provocative words. Alexandra's shadow loomed large as she moved closer to the screen. Everyone held their breath, anxious to see what she would do next.

I had a very bad feeling. "She's going to try something, McGoo."

"I think you're right, Shamble." We both lurched to our feet while the audience members behind us booed for us to sit down and stop blocking the view.

Robin was disturbed and angry. "She wouldn't dare. This will ruin her case! I worked so hard—"

"She doesn't care about her case!" I yelled at her. "And cover your eyes!"

The Medusa turned sideways to the screen that faced the judges. "Tonight you will behold the real Alexandra and remember me for all time!" She spread her arms.

McGoo and I both jumped over the row of seats in front of us to land in the open area before the stage. Spotting a white figure in the shadows behind the curtains backstage,

I realized that it was a statue, a hunchback stagehand who had been petrified while grasping the thick ropes. Alexandra had gotten to him just after he raised the velvet curtains high.

The Medusa's silhouette grabbed the cloth screen facing the panel of judges, extending her well-manicured claws to rip through the fabric. Robin stood up, yelling, "No, Alexandra! Don't!"

But the Medusa shoved the wooden frames, and they all began to topple. In seconds, her hideous visage would be exposed for the judges and the entire audience to see.

Acting instinctively, I did what came first to mind. I pulled my .38 and fired off a shot, even though I didn't have time to aim. Instead of killing Alexandra, which might have saved hundreds of people in the audience, the bullet went wide and struck the petrified hunchback stage-hand. It ricocheted, then *whanged* up to sever the heavy rope that held the scaffolding. The curtains came crashing down, folds of thick velvet plunging like a blood-red waterfall. It blocked the entire stage from the audience.

From behind the curtain, though, I heard the panel of judges cry out, then suddenly fall silent.

Sheyenne swooped past as McGoo and I rushed forward. I yanked off my fedora and covered my face against accidental Alexandra-gazing. Following my lead, McGoo placed his patrolman's cap in front of his own face. Unfortunately, this made it impossible for us to see where we were going, and we tripped over each other as we hit the stairs leading up to the stage.

"This way!" Sheyenne flitted directly through the red

velvet barrier. Following her voice, we raced up the steps and fought our way to the curtain. Behind the red velvet, I heard the struggle as Sheyenne used her poltergeist powers to tear the gauzy fabric from the shielding screens.

The Medusa wailed in frustration. "No! They have to see how beautiful I am!" Her voice became muffled, and the snakes on her head hissed and then wheezed, falling silent as if they were being smothered.

"It's all right, Beaux!" Sheyenne called. "It's safe now."

McGoo and I pushed our way behind the red curtain. Onstage, I saw the wooden framework of the fallen screens, but the cloth had been yanked free. Now the gauzy fabric was wrapped in a large muffling wad around Alexandra's head. The Medusa flailed and clawed at it, but Sheyenne kept adding more, covering her face. I could see only the shadows of Alexandra's features, the confined and squirming serpents that sprouted from her head.

I glanced over to the judges' table, dismayed to see Sheila, Eleanor, and Lewis all marble-white statues in their seats, staring with wide eyes, their faces petrified in exclamations of horror. Egnort, though, sat with a huge clay grin and a completely smitten look on his face. "Pretty lady," he said.

McGoo and I hurried forward to help Sheyenne subdue the suspect, and before long Robin also pushed her way behind the curtain. Always resourceful, she had grabbed one of the orchestra's cymbals and held it up as a reflective shield. Looking down at the cymbal-shield, she cried, "Alexandra, what did you do? I worked so hard to give you a chance!"

"I wanted them to see me!" the Medusa said, her voice muffled. "Why can't I be beautiful like everyone else?"

McGoo slapped handcuffs around her wrists. "You're under arrest for the petrification murders of ten young men from the Monster Match dating service, three members of the judges' panel, and attempted murder of all the audience members at the Miss Unnatural pageant."

"No!" Alexandra wailed, muffled behind the gauzy fabric. "I can't help it! It's who I am."

Ignoring his statue colleagues, the golem lumbered around the judges' table toward us. "Very pretty lady. Totally beautiful. I have never seen anyone so beautiful."

Alexandra's struggles ceased. "Did he say I was pretty?"

I looked curiously at the golem. "Why didn't you turn to stone?"

Egnort squeezed the clay of his arm with one set of fat fingers. "Because I am already stone. Squishy stone, but still stone."

"He thought I was pretty," Alexandra said from beneath the head wrapping.

"Not pretty," Egnort said. "I said you were beautiful." I saw that he had carried the tiara with him from the judges' table. Without ceremony, he placed it on the Medusa's cloth-covered head.

"*Awww,*" Sheyenne said.

McGoo and I hauled Alexandra to her feet. Even though she was being arrested for multiple murders, she seemed more amazed that the golem found her attractive.

Robin sighed. "You're probably going to jail, Alexandra."

"I don't care. Somebody thinks I'm pretty."

The golem adjusted her symbolic tiara and awkwardly put a big clay arm around the Medusa's shoulder. "Can I come see you in prison?"

"I'd really like that," said Alexandra.

"And I thought our romance was weird," I muttered to Sheyenne.

McGoo hustled the stumbling Medusa past the petrified hunchback. "We better add the murder of this stagehand to the charges. I have to start writing this down so I don't forget."

Rattled, Robin shook her head. "I was trying to do what was right."

"You always try to do what's right," I told her. "That's what I like about you. But sometimes *theoretically* right is altogether different from *practical* right."

The golem looked forlornly after them.

From the other side of the curtain, we could hear the audience stirring, beginning to suspect this was not part of the actual pageant.

I went to the rope, disentangled it from the hunchback's stone hand, and began tugging. After I lifted one side of the red velvet curtain, the audience could see part of the stage and the three petrified judges.

"Sorry folks," I said. "The judges are still deliberating. Please go home. It might take them a while."

The zombie ushers filed forward to organize the herd-like movement as the crowd flowed toward the exits.

Robin called out to the departing audience from the stage. "The results of the pageant don't matter. You're all beautiful in your own way. You know it!" Only a few turned around to look at her.

Sheyenne drifted up to me, and I slipped my around her tingling ectoplasmic waist, then I reached out my other arm to put it around Robin's shoulder.

"I know that," I said. "And you two are as beautiful as I can handle."

PREVIOUS PUBLICATION INFORMATION

ABOUT THE AUTHOR

 **Kevin J. Anderson** has published more than 175 books, 58 of which have been national or international bestsellers. He has written numerous novels in the Star Wars, X-Files, and Dune universes, as well as unique steampunk fantasy novels *Clockwork Angels* and *Clockwork Lives*, written with legendary rock drummer Neil Peart. His original works include the Saga of Seven Suns series, the Wake the Dragon and Terra Incognita fantasy trilogies, the Saga of Shadows trilogy, and his humorous horror series featuring Dan Shamble, Zombie PI. He has edited numerous anthologies, written comics and games, and the lyrics to two rock CDs. Anderson is the director of the graduate program in Publishing at Western Colorado University. Anderson and his wife Rebecca Moesta are the publishers of WordFire Press. His most recent novels are *Gods and Dragons*, *Dune: The Duke of Caladan* (with Brian Herbert), *Stake*, *Kill Zone* (with Doug Beason), and *Spine of the Dragon*.

facebook.com/KJAauthor
twitter.com/@TheKJA

Read All the Cases of
Dan Shamble, Zombie P.I.

CPSIA information can be obtained
at www.ICGtesting.com
Printed in the USA
BVHW070324040622
638839BV00003B/19